450

PUFFIN CANADA

CAMP 30

ERIC WALTERS is the author of thirty-two acclaimed and bestselling novels for children and young adults. His novels have won numerous awards, including the Silver Birch, Blue Heron, Red Maple, Snow Willow, Ruth Schwartz and Tiny Torgi, and have received honours from the Canadian Library Association Book Awards and UNESCO's international award for Literature in Service of Tolerance. *Run,* his novel about Terry Fox and the Marathon of Hope, has been a bestseller. *Camp 30* is the sequel to *Camp X*.

Eric resides in Mississauga with his wife, Anita, and children, Christina, Nicholas and Julia. When not writing or touring across the country speaking to school groups, Eric spends time playing or watching soccer and basketball, or playing the saxophone.

To find out more about Eric and his novels, or to arrange for him to speak at your school, visit his website at **www.interlog.com/~ewalters**.

D0089675

Also by Eric Walters from Penguin Canada

The Bully Boys
The Hydrofoil Mystery
Trapped in Ice
Camp X
Royal Ransom
Run

Other books by Eric Walters

Overdrive
I've Got an Idea
Underdog
Death by Exposure
Road Trip
Northern Exposures
Long Shot
Tiger in Trouble
Hoop Crazy
Rebound
Full Court Press
Caged Eagles
The Money Pit Mystery
Three-on-Three
Visions
Tiger by the Tail
War of the Eagles
Stranded
Diamonds in the Rough
STARS
Stand Your Ground

CAMP 30

ERIC WALTERS

PUFFIN
CANADA

PUFFIN CANADA

Published by the Penguin Group

Penguin Group (Canada), 10 Alcorn Avenue, Toronto, Ontario, Canada M4V 3B2
    (a division of Pearson Penguin Canada Inc.)

Penguin Group (USA) Inc., 375 Hudson Street, New York, New York 10014, U.S.A.

Penguin Books Ltd, 80 Strand, London WC2R 0RL, England

Penguin Ireland, 25 St Stephen's Green, Dublin 2, Ireland (a division of Penguin Books Ltd)

Penguin Group (Australia), 250 Camberwell Road, Camberwell, Victoria 3124, Australia
    (a division of Pearson Australia Group Pty Ltd)

Penguin Books India Pvt Ltd, 11 Community Centre, Panchsheel Park,
    New Delhi – 110 017, India

Penguin Group (NZ), Cnr Airborne and Rosedale Roads, Albany, Auckland, New Zealand
    (a division of Pearson New Zealand Ltd)

Penguin Books (South Africa) (Pty) Ltd, 24 Sturdee Avenue, Rosebank, Johannesburg 2196,
    South Africa

Penguin Books Ltd, Registered Offices: 80 Strand, London WC2R 0RL, England

First published in a Viking Canada hardcover by Penguin Group (Canada),
    a division of Pearson Penguin Canada Inc., 2004
Published in this edition, 2004

(OPM) 10 9 8 7 6 5 4 3 2 1

LIBRARY AND ARCHIVES CANADA CATALOGUING IN PUBLICATION

Walters, Eric, 1957–
    Camp 30 / Eric Walters.

Sequel to: Camp X.
For children aged 8–12.
ISBN 0-14-301678-4

1. Camp 30 (Bowmanville, Ont.)—Juvenile fiction. 2. World War, 1939–1945—Prisoners and
prisons, Canadian—Juvenile fiction. 3. Prisoners of war—Germany—Juvenile fiction.
4. Prisoners of war—Canada—Juvenile fiction. I. Title. II. Title: Camp Thirty.

PS8595.A598C35 2004a   jC813'.54   C2004-906157-7

Visit the Penguin Group (Canada) website at **www.penguin.ca**

For my good friend Lynn-Phillip Hodgson, who is not only the world expert on Camp X and Camp 30, but gave me both his encouragement and expertise in creating this novel

CAMP 30

CHAPTER ONE

"GREAT SHOT, JACK!" I exclaimed as the newspaper skittered across the porch and bumped into the front door of the house.

"I'm getting to be as good with my left arm as I am with my right," Jack said. Good thing, too, because my brother's right arm was encased in plaster to allow his broken wrist to mend.

"You do the next one," he offered.

"Sure." I was trying to sound confident even though I wasn't. I pulled a paper out of the bag slung over my shoulder, folded it, cocked my arm and let it fly. The paper flew end over end, slammed into the porch railing and fell back into the bushes.

"You throw like a girl," Jack said.

"Shut up!" I snapped. I walked across the grass,

1

retrieved the paper and tossed it over the railing and onto the porch.

"Maybe I should call you Georgia instead of George."

"I'm telling you to shut up!"

"And just what are you gonna do to make me?"

That was a good question. My brother wasn't just older, he was bigger and tougher, too.

"You gonna tell Mommy on me? You gonna tell her that I was mean to her little baby boy—I mean, baby girl?" He laughed at his lame joke and then reached over to tweak my cheek. I knocked his hand away.

"Oh, so you want to fight me, do you?"

He dropped his newspaper bag to the pavement and started bouncing around, fists out like a prizefighter.

"I can take you with one hand tied behind my back!" He put his broken hand behind him. "Does little Georgie think he's a tough guy now 'cause he's just turned twelve? I'm still your big brother and I'll always be your big brother!"

"You'll always be two years older than me but that doesn't mean you'll always be two years bigger than me."

"Ooh! That sounds like a threat," Jack replied, and he jabbed me in the shoulder. It hurt but I tried not to react.

"Maybe I should knock you around now before you get so *big and tough* that I won't be able to." He laughed and punched me again.

"Stop it now!" I yelled. I was used to this kind of teasing from my brother, but I wasn't really in the mood for it.

"Or what, Georgie?"

"Or this." I slipped the newspaper bag off my shoulder and let it drop to the ground. "Deliver your own papers." I turned and walked away.

"Come on, George, I was just goofing around!"

I kept walking.

"Don't be such a baby!"

I didn't even slow down.

"Okay ... you win!"

Now I stopped and turned around. "Win what?" I asked.

"I won't do it again," he said. I started to walk back. "At least I won't do it again *today*."

That was what I'd expected. It was good enough for now. I picked up the bag and slung it back over my shoulder. We walked along again in silence. It was a hot day— a real scorcher—and we were nowhere near done.

"You're awful quiet today," Jack said.

"Just thinking."

"That's a first."

I shot him a dirty look.

"So what were you thinking about?" Jack asked.

"I was thinking about how all of this is pretty strange."

"Delivering papers is strange?" Jack asked as he tossed another paper up onto a porch. I wished *he* would hit the bushes every now and again.

"Yeah."

"How do you figure that? We're on the same route, same houses, delivering the same paper we always do," Jack said.

"That's what's so strange," I replied.

Jack shot me a my-brother-is-an-idiot look.

"Just think. After everything that's gone on over the last few weeks—all those things that nobody would believe even if we could tell them—here we are acting like absolutely nothing happened. It's like it was all just a dream."

"Maybe for you. I carry around a reminder everywhere I go," he said, holding up his arm. "And every time I look in a mirror or try to eat anything."

"How is your jaw?"

"Better, but still not perfect, not by a long shot."

Jack's jaw had been fractured at the same time his wrist had been broken.

"But think about it," I continued. "Here we are delivering the *Whitby Reporter,* the paper that Mr. Krum used to own, and now he's dead, and—"

"He's lucky he *is* dead or he'd have to deal with me!"

"Or Bill or Little Bill or the other agents at Camp X."

"Keep your voice down!" Jack cautioned.

I looked around. "There's nobody to hear me. Besides, talking to you is the only thing that reminds me it was real."

"Then just don't talk about that stinking Krum! He was nothing more than a Nazi, a traitor, a spy!"

Jack took another paper and heaved it onto the porch of the next house. This time it smashed against the door with a thunderous crash. The glass at the top of the door rattled and shook, and for an instant I thought it might shatter.

"You almost put that one *through* the door," I said.

"At least I hit the door instead of the railing or the—"

"Young man!" We turned back around. A woman—an old, wrinkled woman who was probably at least seventy—was poking her head out of the door Jack had just hit with the paper.

"Do you realize that you nearly scared me half to death?" she called out.

"Sorry, ma'am," Jack said. "It sort of got away from me. I'm not so good with my left hand." He held up his right arm to show her the cast.

"I nearly jumped right out of my skin. It sounded like somebody shooting at my house."

Jack and I exchanged a look. It had been loud, but nothing like a gunshot. We knew, from right up close, what that sounded like.

"I imagine I should just be grateful to be getting my paper again," she continued.

After Mr. Krum's death the paper hadn't been

published for two weeks. Then, on the front cover of the
first new issue, was the story about how he'd died.

"I was so saddened to hear about the publisher's death
in that automobile accident," she said. "Mr. Krum was
such a nice man."

Without looking I sensed my brother stiffening beside
me. I knew he wanted to say something—about how
Krum had *really* died, about what sort of man he *really*
was—but he couldn't. He was—*we* were—sworn to
secrecy under the Official Secrets Act.

"Say ... your arm ... Were you one of the boys in the
car? I heard that two of Mr. Krum's paper boys were in
the car with him when he died."

"We were both in the car," I lied. Neither of us had
been in the car with Mr. Krum when he'd died, because
he hadn't really died in a car crash.

"How awful for the two of you!" she exclaimed.
"Thank the good Lord that you both survived." She
paused. "I heard it was mechanical failure, that something
went wrong with his steering."

"That's what we were told," Jack said.

"I'm sorry for raising my voice like that," she said.
"You boys have been through a lot ... I was just so
startled by the sound. My Harold—my son—says I'm
as nervous as a cat in a room full of rocking chairs. It
hasn't made it any easier with him serving overseas.
He's fighting in Africa."

"Our dad is there, too," I said. "He's with the St. Patrick's Regiment."

"I'm sure you're as proud of him as I am of my Harold. But pride doesn't chase away the worry, does it?"

She was right about that.

"And it doesn't make my nerves any better to hear about all those strange goings-on up at Glenrath," she continued.

I felt a chill go up my spine.

"Glenrath?" Jack asked, trying to sound innocent and ignorant. "What's that?"

"Your family's not from around these parts, are they?"

"We've only been here a couple of months," I answered. "We moved down here from our farm so our mother could work at the big D.I.L. munitions plant in Ajax."

"Lots and lots of newcomers here in Whitby since the war. To us old-timers the Sinclair farm is called Glenrath. It's down by the lake, right by Thornton Road. The Sinclairs pulled up stakes and sold it, must be nearly a year ago now."

"Don't know it," Jack said, pretending.

"And you haven't heard about any of the commotion around there?"

We both shook our heads.

"Explosions, planes coming and going, lots of strangers. I heard it was some kind of secret training place for spies, that's what I heard." She said the last few words so softly that her voice was barely audible.

"That's pretty hard to believe," Jack said.

"I've heard stories," she said. "Maybe it's only gossip, but there's often truth in gossip."

"We haven't heard anything at all," I said.

"Nothing?" she asked. "Not a thing?"

I shrugged, and Jack shook his head.

She started to chuckle. "Funny, you two are delivering the news but you know a lot less than anybody else in town."

She'd have been shocked to find out what we really did know—probably a lot more than anybody else in Whitby!

"I guess we're just too busy working to spend time wagging our tongues," Jack said.

The amused expression on her face was gone now—she looked as though she'd just bitten into something sour.

"We have more papers to deliver. Good morning, ma'am."

Jack turned and started away. I gave the old woman a wave goodbye and hurried after him.

"Stupid old biddy," Jack said as I reached his side.

"That was strange."

Jack shot me another look.

"I mean her wanting to talk about the camp."

"Other than the weather and the war, what else is there to talk about around here?"

"It reminded me of the way Mr. Krum always tried to pump us for information, that's all."

Jack burst out laughing. "So you think that the old woman is a German spy too?"

"She could be!" I said defiantly. "You never can tell."

Jack stopped snickering. "You know, considering all we've been through, I guess maybe you're right."

"I am?" I asked, shocked that Jack was agreeing with me.

"I've learned the hard way that things aren't always what you think they are."

"So you think she *could* be a German spy?"

"She could be Adolf Hitler's mother for all I know."

It was my turn to laugh.

"More likely she's a spy for *our* side, though," Jack went on.

"What do you mean?"

"Maybe she was told to talk to us to see if we'd reveal anything about Camp X, if we'd break the Official Secrets Act."

"We'd never do that!"

"I know that, but maybe Bill doesn't," Jack said.

"Bill trusts us," I argued. Bill was military, in charge of security at Camp X. We'd gotten to know him pretty well after blundering into the camp and landing in a load of trouble.

"It really doesn't matter if he trusts us or not as long as we don't say any—" Jack stopped mid-sentence as a familiar-looking white panel truck slowly passed us, moving up the street. At the intersection it came to a stop, flashing its tail lights, and then turned to the right, disappearing behind a stand of trees.

I turned to Jack. "Is that the same truck?" We'd been seeing it—or one just like it—all over the neighbourhood.

"Maybe, maybe not. Even if it is, it doesn't necessarily mean anything."

"But did you notice how slowly it was driving when it passed us this time?"

"It was probably looking for a number on one of the houses," Jack said. "Whitby's a small town. It's probably just a coincidence."

"Well," I said, "I'm going to keep my eyes open and just see if—"

We both saw the truck as we turned the corner. It was pulled over, a hundred feet down the road.

"Another coincidence?" I asked.

"One more than I like. Come on, let's go straight ahead up the street."

"But we have to deliver some papers down that way," I said, gesturing toward where the truck was parked.

"We'll come back for them at the end of the route."

I knew it meant a longer walk, but I wasn't going to argue. We started to cross the street. I looked at the truck. It was covered with dust and dirt, and the window was up despite the heat, and—

"Owww!" I howled as Jack punched me in the shoulder. My head spun around. "Why did you do that?"

"Don't look at it," Jack ordered. "If they *are* looking at us, we don't want them to see us looking at them."

"Why not?"

"Figure it out for yourself!" he snapped.

What I figured was that maybe Jack was getting even more paranoid than me. What I knew for sure, though, was that Jack was mostly right—and even when he wasn't right he was still bigger than me. And I didn't want another punch.

We crossed the road and continued up the street. If the truck reappeared now it would be a whole lot more than just a couple of coincidences.

"Third house in on the other side gets a paper," Jack said.

"Oh, yeah, right." I dug a paper out of the bag and started across the street. Looking back, I was relieved to see the empty road. No panel truck ... not even a kid on a bike. I trotted up the front walkway, getting close enough to the house to make sure my toss landed on the porch. I threw, and the paper skidded into the door. I started back across the street, looking both ways, and there it was—a white panel truck coming down the road toward us from the direction we were heading.

"Jack?"

"I see it. Get over here."

I scrambled to his side. "Is it the same one?" I asked.

"I can't tell. Maybe."

The panel truck moved slowly down the street. The sun was reflecting off the windshield and I couldn't see who was driving or if there was anybody in the passenger seat. It slowed down even more and came to a stop right beside us. I slid over so Jack was between it and me. Then the window rolled down and a young woman stuck her head partway out.

"Excuse me!" she called. She had a heavy accent ... but it wasn't German. French, maybe. "Do you boys know where is King Street?"

"That's in the centre of the village," Jack answered. "Go back down to Highway 2, turn left and you'll find it."

"What is ... *highway*?" the woman asked.

"It's a big road," Jack said, "with lots of cars. And when you get there, go that way," Jack said, pointing to his left.

"Ah," the woman said, nodding her head and flashing a big, friendly smile. She was very pretty. "Could you show me on this map?" she asked, holding it up and partway out the window.

"Sure, easy," Jack said, smiling back. He walked across the road to the driver's-side window. I trailed behind him. I think we were both feeling a little silly about our earlier suspicions.

"It's not hard," Jack said. He took the map from her hands. "You just take this road right here and then——"

Out of nowhere two men dressed in black raced around the side of the truck. "Both of you, not a word!" one of them warned. The two men pinned us against the side of the vehicle.

"Into the truck!" one of them ordered. I looked down. There was a pistol in his hand!

CHAPTER TWO

THE WOMAN BEHIND THE WHEEL opened her door and stepped out. The man grabbed me by the arm and started to push me forward. I resisted—until he shoved the pistol into my back. Then I climbed in behind the wheel and was grabbed by a second set of arms and pulled over the seat and—

"Bill!" I exclaimed.

"How nice of you to drop in," he said. He sat in the middle seat, a smile on his face.

"I'm so glad to see—"

"Leave me alone!" Jack screamed as he was thrown into the truck, crashing into me and knocking me over.

"It's Bill, Jack! It's Bill!" I yelled.

Jack struggled to untangle his limbs from mine and got to his knees. He looked shocked, surprised, and confused—and angry, to boot.

"You two should make yourselves comfortable. Sit," he

said, patting the seat beside him.

We pulled ourselves up and onto the seat. Just then the side door of the truck opened and the two men climbed in, slamming the door closed behind them.

"These are my associates," Bill said as the two younger men took places on the back seat.

"Pleased to meet you." One of them extended his hand over the seat and shook first Jack's hand and then mine. The second man did the same. Both had heavy foreign accents.

The truck's engine roared to life. I turned back around. The driver—the woman—was back behind the wheel. The truck started off, swaying as it pulled away from the side of the road.

"So you must be wondering why you're here," Bill said.

"That sort of crossed my mind," I admitted.

"And why did you have to get us this way?" Jack asked. "Why didn't you just call us instead of staging a kidnapping?"

"The original plan was to call you," Bill said, "later on today. Until we noticed that you had broken our surveillance."

"We didn't break it!" I protested. "We haven't touched anything!"

Bill laughed. "Surveillance. It means we were watching you, and we realized that you'd seen us watching you."

"I told you not to look at them!" Jack snapped.

"That wasn't it," Bill said. "As soon as you started across the street rather than turning right the way you usually do, we knew you were aware of our presence."

"How do you know we usually turn right?" Jack asked.

"Because you've turned right at that intersection every day for the past week delivering your papers."

"But how do you know that?" I asked.

"He told you, George. They've been watching us."

"For the past week?"

"Actually, for the past ten days," Bill explained.

"We only started to get suspicious a couple of days ago," Jack said.

Bill turned around in his seat and looked at the two men. "Some of my operatives seem to be much better than others at observing without being observed."

"Sorry," one of the men mumbled, and the second looked down at his feet.

"But I don't understand why you'd be watching us to begin with," I said.

"Isn't it obvious?" Jack snapped again.

"No. Explain it to me," I challenged him.

"It's probably some sort of training exercise," Jack said. "You've had people watching us to help them learn how to do it, right?"

"Very sharp, Jack," Bill said. Jack puffed out his chest proudly. "At least, that's part of the reason."

Bill leaned forward then and tapped the driver on the shoulder. She turned slightly around in her seat.

"Could you please pull over?" he said.

The truck slowed down, and then I could hear the sound of gravel beneath the tires as it swayed and veered onto the gravel shoulder of the road.

"Everybody get out," Bill said as soon as the truck had rolled to a stop. Nobody moved. "Out!" he yelled, and I tried to get to my feet.

"Not you," he said, putting a hand on my shoulder. "You and Jack stay. Everybody else leaves. It won't take long, but I need to talk to the boys alone."

The driver turned off the engine and climbed out. The two men in the back shuffled to the side door, opened it, got out and closed the door behind them with a loud thud.

"I needed them to leave," Bill told us.

"Because they're foreigners?" Jack jumped in. "I noticed they had accents."

"No, that's got nothing to do with it," Bill said. "A lot of our agents are originally from Europe—from countries that are now our allies, of course. It gives them a tremendous advantage if they find themselves parachuted in to their home countries. I sent them away simply because they're not authorized to hear what I'm going to say."

"But we are?" I asked.

"You know more about our operations than most of the spies we're training. Besides, there's not much choice, since this involves you two ... you two and your mother."

"Our mother? Is she okay?" Suddenly I was feeling scared again.

"She's fine. Actually, probably better than fine." He looked at his watch. "Right about now your mother will be very happy. She's being offered a new job, which will involve a promotion and a significant raise and—"

"That's fantastic!" I exclaimed.

"And a relocation," Bill continued.

"Relocation? What does that mean?"

"A move. Your family will be leaving Whitby so your mother can take the new position. The job is in Bowmanville."

"Where's that?" Jack asked.

"Not far. It's a small town about twenty miles east of here. Very nice little town. I'm sure you'll enjoy it."

"Did you arrange for the new job?" Jack asked.

"Not me personally, although I knew they were looking for a position for your mother that would involve a relocation."

"But why do you want us to leave Whitby?" I asked. "We already promised we wouldn't go near the camp again unless you asked us. You gotta believe us."

"I do believe you. I know you and Jack are men of your word. This is a safety issue ... I'd better explain." He took a deep breath and then let out an equally loud sigh. "I'm not sure how much you know—or how much I really should be telling you—but we monitor the airways, taking in random radio transmissions."

"That's what the radio towers are for, right?" I asked. At the camp there was a series of gigantic towers, webbed with wire, that sent and received radio messages. We were told that they could get messages from as far away as Europe.

Bill nodded. "Twelve days ago we intercepted a Nazi message, a *coded* message, a message that we believe originated in this general area."

"Does that mean that there are still German spies operating around here?"

"They have spies here, George, just as we have spies in Nazi-controlled Europe. They are operating throughout the country."

"And you want our help to find them?" Jack asked. He sounded as though he couldn't wait.

"I'm afraid it's quite the opposite. I want your help in keeping them away from you."

"I don't get it," Jack said, voicing what I was thinking.

"The message that we intercepted mentioned two brothers and Camp X," Bill explained.

"Us?" I gasped. "They mentioned us in a secret message?"

"We're not certain it has anything to do with you two," Bill said. "Most likely it refers to something completely unrelated. There are dozens of different possible interpretations."

"But you think it might have something to do with us, or you wouldn't be here to begin with," Jack said.

"There's a chance, and even if it's a very small chance, we mustn't gamble with your lives."

"Our lives?" I gulped. "You think that they could … they could …?"

Bill didn't answer right away. My gut tightened into a knot.

"I'm not going to lie to you. You know these people mean business. They're cold, calculating killers."

The knot in my stomach grew larger. I thought back to that deserted farmhouse, my brother and I tied to those chairs, and Mr. Krum holding that gun under orders to kill us.

"There have been deaths caused by Nazi agents," Bill said.

"Around here?"

"As close as Toronto. Two weeks ago. A woman training as an operative was shot … bullet to the back of the head. It wasn't a robbery—her purse wasn't even touched. Cold, clean assassination."

"That's awful." A shudder went through my entire body.

"That's why the two of you and your mother have been under constant surveillance since the message was decoded. We wanted to take all necessary steps to protect you. But you have to know that we can't keep that many operatives employed watching your family day and night," Bill said. "And that's why we've arranged this new job and new location for your family."

"And we'll be safe there?" I asked.

"You'll be safe. Nobody in Bowmanville will know you. We're going to hide you in plain sight."

"Does our mother know anything about this?" Jack asked. "I mean, about why we're moving?"

"Nothing," Bill said. "As far as she's concerned, it's simply a better job, with better pay, in a new town. She knows nothing of this, as she has known nothing of anything that's happened to you two."

"I guess that's better," Jack said. "There's no point in worrying her."

"When do we leave?" I asked.

"Your mother starts her new job on Monday morning."

"But that's only four days from now!" I exclaimed.

"She'll have help packing and moving. It's essential that we proceed as quickly and quietly as possible," Bill explained. "I hope you understand—we had no choice."

"We know you're only doing what's best for us," Jack told him. "And it isn't like this is our home anyway. We've only been here a few months."

"I'm glad you see it that way," Bill said. "Now, I better let the two of you get back to delivering your papers. Your mother will be home shortly. Do try to look surprised when she tells you the good news."

CHAPTER THREE

"THAT'S THE LAST OF THEM," I said as I dropped the box onto the kitchen floor—the kitchen of our new house.

"You two must be exhausted!" Mom said.

"We hardly did anything. Especially me," Jack said, holding up his cast. "You were the one up all night packing these boxes. All we had to do was help move them, and there was lots of help doing that."

It was true.

A big gray army truck and a half-dozen soldiers had arrived to help us move, courtesy of Colonel Armstrong, our mother's new boss. The whole house had been loaded, and then unloaded, in only a few short hours.

"Well, you both did a wonderful job. And this certainly is a lovely old house," my mother said, looking around.

"It reminds me of home," I said. Jack and I had grown up on the family farm, but with Dad off fighting in the war we couldn't go on working the property. That was why we'd moved to Whitby in the first place, so Mom could take a job at the big D.I.L. plant, making ammunition for the war.

"I know what I like best about the new place," Jack said.

"What?" I asked.

"Separate bedrooms. I won't have to share a room with you!" he said, pointing at me.

"I'm the one who should be happy. At least I know how to hang up my clothes, and I'm not the one who snores!"

"I don't—!"

"Both of you, stop it!" our mother ordered. "Can't you two ever have a discussion without fighting?"

"We *could*," I said.

"Yeah, it might happen … someday … maybe," Jack agreed.

"Rather than fighting, how about if you two go out and explore a little?" she suggested.

Jack shook his head. "We should stay here and help unpack."

"If you really want to help me get things straightened away, the two of you should go out and leave me in peace."

"So you're saying the best way we can help is not to help?" I asked.

"At least not right away. I need time to think and a cup of tea to help calm my nerves."

"But we can't just leave you here working while we're doing nothing," I said.

She reached over and gave me a kiss on the cheek, and then did the same to Jack. "There are going to be a couple of very lucky girls who land my boys someday."

"Mom ..." I protested.

"Actually, there is something you could do for me," she said.

"What?" Jack asked.

"I'm going to be walking to work every day, and I don't know exactly how long it's going to take me. You boys could walk there and let me know."

"We *could* do that," I said.

"Although it still sounds more like a way to get us out of your hair than anything else," Jack pointed out.

"It's both. Will you do it?"

"Yeah, sure," I said, and Jack shrugged in agreement.

"Good. You'll have to walk through town, head out along Church Street and go east."

"You're not working in town?" I asked.

"No, about a mile and a half or two east."

"That's a fair distance to walk."

"Hopefully I'll be able to get a ride some days. I was told that many of the people I'll be working with live here in Bowmanville."

"That's good. Are you sure we'll be able to find this place today?" I asked.

"That shouldn't be a problem. I was told it's a new wooden building. Just beside it will be high fences topped with barbed wire and even taller guard towers."

"Barbed wire ... guard towers?" I questioned.

"Pretty standard for a prisoner-of-war camp. Didn't I tell you that's where I'll be working?"

"No, you didn't!" I gasped.

"I guess it just sort of slipped my mind in all the confusion. Colonel Armstrong is the commander of a prisoner-of-war camp."

"Camp 30," I said.

"Yes, that's right. I guess I *did* mention it."

Jack shot me an angry look. Mom hadn't said anything. We'd known about it longer than she had because Mr. Krum had told us. Of course *he'd* known—he was a spy, after all. But it was classified information to civilians, and I was going to have to do some fast talking to explain myself.

Jack jumped to my rescue. "Sure, you mentioned it. We just didn't know it was a P.O.W. camp, that's all."

"There are prisoner-of-war camps throughout Canada, but this one is particularly important," our mother said. "The highest-ranking German officers captured in the war are prisoners there."

"How many prisoners are there?" Jack asked.

"I'm not really supposed to say much," she answered. "I had to sign some papers saying I'd keep information quiet."

"The Official Secrets Act," I said.

"Yes, that's it! How did you know?"

I didn't even look at Jack, because I knew angry eyes would be staring back at me. "I read all about it in the newspapers. We don't just deliver the paper, you know. I read it all the time."

"I had to swear not to say anything about my work. I could be fined or go to jail," she said. "But I guess I can say a few things to my two boys … as long as they don't say anything to anybody else."

"We wouldn't," I said.

"Yeah, we're good at keeping secrets … well, at least one of us is."

"And just what secrets have you been keeping?" my mother asked Jack suspiciously. It was my turn to shoot him the evil eye. But she must have decided to let him off the hook, because she went on to answer his original question.

"I understand there are close to 650 prisoners in the camp."

"It's scary to think there are that many Nazis that close to us," I said.

"Just remember, they're inside the fence—actually, inside *two* barbed-wire fences—and there are guards with guns who make sure that they stay there. I was told that there have been no successful escapes."

"So that must mean there have been *un*successful

attempts," I reasoned. "The prisoners must be trying to escape all the time."

"What's the point in even trying?" Jack asked. "Germany is one heck of a long hike and then a swim across the Atlantic Ocean."

"That's exactly why they moved the prisoners all the way to Canada," my mother added. "I just don't want you boys worrying about me all day. I'm going to be perfectly safe."

It all made sense. She'd be surrounded all day by soldiers and guards with guns, so that was a great place for her, a safe place to be.

"Now, why don't you two go and have a look at the camp? And remember, don't walk too fast. I want to know how long it's going to take *me* to get there."

"There it is," I said. Up ahead on the left-hand side of the road I could see a high wooden tower rising into the sky. Behind it, faint but still visible, was the outline of a fence, almost as tall.

"So that's where they keep all the stinking Nazis they capture," Jack said ominously.

"If Krum had been captured instead of killed, would they have put him there?"

"Doubt it. Mom said it was for soldiers, not spies. Spies they just shoot, I think."

"Really?"

"Bullet to the back of the brain," Jack said as he pressed a finger against the base of my skull.

I brushed his hand away. "They don't do that," I said.

"Mr. Krum was going to do that to us," he argued.

"But that's because he was a Nazi. We treat people fairly."

Jack laughed. "There's no *fair* in war. You fight evil with evil."

I wanted to ask, If that was the case, what made us better than them to begin with? but I didn't. I knew that war was a dirty business, and maybe sometimes you had to do things you didn't necessarily want to do.

It had taken us about twenty-five minutes to get there, walking through town and then east along a dirt road with farmers' fields on either side. The camp itself was in the middle of some scrub, a good distance from any farmhouse. As we continued to walk, the features of the camp became clearer. On one side of the road were a few small, ordinary-looking places—maybe offices. But on the other side there were buildings—dozens of brick buildings—behind a fence. Linking the buildings were concrete walkways, and along the walkways, as well as in front of many of the buildings, were beds filled with bright, beautiful flowers. It wasn't what I'd expected a prisoner-of-war camp to look like.

Just as Mom had said, there were two fences, running parallel, about fifteen feet apart. On the top of both fences were strands of barbed wire, and every few yards there was a light.

Up ahead, outside the fence, stood one of the tall guard towers—I counted nine different towers in all. Stairs led up to an open-sided, roofed area, like a turret. I caught a glimpse of a man peering out at the camp.

"Look, there's some Nazis right there!" Jack exclaimed.

Four men in German uniforms were walking along one of the paths, moving very quickly. We stopped and gawked until they reached the building and disappeared inside.

"Our dad could have been the one who captured them," I said.

"Not unless he's been rowing a boat across the African desert."

"What?"

"Didn't you look at the uniforms? Those weren't soldiers, they were sailors."

"Oh … I didn't notice."

"Obviously," Jack said.

We continued along the road past the guard tower. We turned when we came to a cross street and continued to circle the camp.

"If there are hundreds of prisoners, how come we've only seen four?" I asked. "The place looks deserted."

"Deserted, but awfully fancy. I didn't think a prisoner-of-war camp would have such nice buildings ... and flowers. What's with the flowers?"

"That is strange," I admitted. "I thought it would be just dirt and— Did you hear that?" I asked.

Jack nodded. "It sounds like a crowd ... yelling ... or cheering."

"Yeah, but that doesn't make any sense at all."

We heard it again. It *did* sound like cheering. As we continued down the road, the noise got louder and louder. Then, up ahead, we saw where it was coming from. Behind the fence there was a soccer game going on! There were men, all in shorts, one side dressed in blue, the other in brown, racing up and down a soccer pitch. And on the far side of the field were spectators— hundreds and hundreds of spectators—cheering on the players. We drifted over toward the fence to see.

As we watched, one of the players made a dash down the side of the field. He moved past one player and then a second, and then put a high, arching cross to the front of the net. The goalie came charging out to get the ball, but a split second before he arrived another player got his head on it and the ball soared over the goalie and into the net. Jack and I joined in as the crowd roared its approval.

"That was amazing!" Jack yelled. "Amazing!"

"It was an outstanding play," a voice called out.

Jack and I looked at each other and then for the source of the voice.

"That was his third goal of the match."

Just inside the fence, leaning against a tree, stood a man—a soldier, a Nazi.

"That makes the score four goals to two," he continued. His English was perfect, but there was an obvious accent—a German accent.

"The blue team is the Luftwaffe—you would say the air force—while the team in brown represents the African corps of the army."

Africa? Our father could have helped capture *those* guys—he could have been fighting against them!

"I myself cheer for neither of these teams. I am with the navy and will cheer the sea-green team tomorrow. It will be a good match. Are you boys fans of the game?"

Neither of us answered.

"I know my English has become fairly good so I must assume that either you boys do not speak English or you do not wish to speak to a prisoner."

"We speak English," I said.

"Ah, so it is the latter."

"We don't speak to Nazis!" Jack snapped.

The man smiled. "I try to avoid that myself," he said. "I am an officer in the German navy and not a member of the Nazi party. Many people, even some Germans, do not understand the difference between—"

"Hey!" a voice yelled.

We caught sight of movement and looked up to the top of the nearest guard tower. A guard had poked his head out and was gesturing to us.

"You boys gotta move away from the fence!" he yelled. "This isn't a flipping sideshow, you know!"

We quickly backed away.

"It is all right, old man!" the German yelled up at the guard. "They're here to watch soccer, not to help plot my escape!"

"You keep outta this, Fritz, or I'll write you up on report!" the guard retorted.

"The name is Otto, and I doubt you have sufficient education to even know how to write!"

"Come on, let's get out of here," Jack said, grabbing me by the arm. We hurried off down the road, leaving the two men, prisoner and guard, to continue hurling insults at each other.

CHAPTER FOUR

"WHAT WOULD YOU SAY to a soda right now?" Jack asked.

"I'd say, 'Hello, glad to meet you.'" It was hot, and it had been a long walk to the camp and back.

Jack reached into his pocket and pulled out a dime.

"Where'd you get that from?" I asked.

"Mom. She said we should have a treat for being so good about moving again."

"Why shouldn't we be good?" I asked. "It's our fault that we had to move in the first place."

"It all worked out, though. Mom has a better job, she's getting more money, and we get to live in a bigger, nicer house."

"And it's not like we were even in Whitby long enough to make friends," I added. "Besides, it feels good to have Mom working somewhere other than the munitions factory. I was always afraid that something would blow up."

"Me too," Jack said. "Although working close to a bunch of dangerous Nazis maybe isn't the best either."

"Mom said she didn't actually work inside the camp ... I think her office is in one of those little buildings across the road," I said. "Besides, there are those fences, and barbed wire and guard towers and guards and everything. They can't get out."

Jack didn't answer.

"Can they?"

"Probably not. And even if they do, they're going to try to get as far away from the camp as possible, not hang around."

That was reassuring.

"You should only be worrying about one thing right now," Jack said, "and that's whether the soda is cold."

We were walking along one of the main streets in town, and Jack had spotted a tidy little grocery store with a sign advertising cold drinks.

Jack pushed open the door of the store and a bell pinged to announce our entrance.

"Good afternoon, boys," called out a little man from behind the counter. He was small and wrinkled and his voice quavered with age.

"Good afternoon, sir," Jack and I both said.

"Nice manners," the man said. "Not that my eyes see everything so clearly any more, but I don't think I know you two."

"We're new, sir. Just moved in this morning."

"House up on Chestnut, right?" he asked.

"Yeah, that's our place. How did you know?"

He chuckled. "Bowmanville's getting bigger, but it's still not that big. What can I do for you two young fellas?"

"We were hoping for a soda," Jack said.

"A cold soda," I added.

"We have some back this way in the refrigerator." He circled the counter and started for the back of the store. His steps were tiny and halting and his advanced age was even more obvious. Just how old was he?

"What flavour you boys want?"

"Two lemon-limes, please, sir," Jack said.

The old man pulled them out and handed them to us. "Don't know your folks, but they must be good people to raise such polite kids. I'm sure I'll meet 'em soon enough."

"Our father isn't with us," Jack said, and the man's eyebrows went up. "He's fighting in Africa ... he's with the St. Patty's Regiment."

"Good for him! And your mother?"

"We came here because she got a new job," Jack said. "She's going to be working at Camp 30 as an assistant to the colonel who runs the place."

"That would be Colonel Armstrong. My son tells me he's a good fella."

"Your son?" I asked.

"Yep, he works up there. He's one of the guards."

"The guards?" Jack looked at me, and I knew we were thinking the same thing.

"Um ... I don't mean any offence, sir, but I was just wondering, wouldn't your son be a little bit old to be a guard?" Jack asked.

"All the guards are part of the V.G.C., the Veteran Guards of Canada. Men who served king and country in other wars but are too old to fight in this one. My son was a soldier in World War I."

"That was a long time ago," I said.

"Doesn't seem that long ago to me. Less than twenty-five years. Some of the V.G.C. soldiers fought in the Boer War, which goes back before that."

"When was the Boer War?" I asked.

"Aren't they teaching you kids any history?" he asked. "That's what's wrong with schools today, not teaching kids about their own past. The Boer War was fought in South Africa. Began in 1899 and ended—with the British Empire triumphant—in 1902. Some of them soldiers are grandfathers many times over now."

Somehow having grandfathers as guards didn't seem like a good thing to me. After all, these were the people keeping the prisoners away from my mother!

"My son is a young fella compared to some. He's just turned fifty."

"Is there an age limit for the job?" Jack asked.

"Officially it's fifty-five, but I know a few of these fellas and they haven't seen fifty-five for a long, long time, believe me!" He laughed. "Maybe I should turn in my shopkeeper's apron for a rifle myself. Pay's not bad, and the hours would be a sight better than what I work here."

He turned and shuffled his way back to the counter. We followed.

"That'll be eight cents," he said, and my brother handed him the dime. He pushed a button on the cash register, it rang loudly and the cash drawer opened. He dropped in the dime and pulled out two pennies, handing them to my brother.

"You let your mother know that I can offer her good prices on all canned goods—I just wish I had more to offer. Don't have the variety we once had," he said, gesturing around the store. Some of the shelves were only half full, and a couple were completely empty. "The war's made a lot of things hard to get."

"That's okay. It's that way for everybody everywhere, sir," I said.

"Not everybody," he said. "Not for the prisoners up at the camp."

We both gave him a confused look.

"They get whatever they want. Fresh fruit and vegetables, sugar, good portions of meat, cigarettes and even beer!"

"The prisoners get beer?" Jack asked in astonishment.

"Four different types they get to choose from, and that's not even to mention the alcohol they brew for themselves in secret stills right there in the camp. There's no shortage of anything for them."

"But that can't be … that isn't fair," I said.

"Not fair, indeed, but that's the way it is. Sometimes gets my son all bothered to think that the prisoners are getting more than the guards. Makes him wonder who the prisoners really are."

"That doesn't make any sense," Jack said.

"You're right, it doesn't make any sense. Something called the Geneva Convention says we have to treat prisoners well. I doubt they're treating our boys so well when they get captured!"

"Why would we be treating a bunch of stinking Nazis better than we get treated?" Jack asked.

"Lots of things that don't make sense to me," the old man said. "The older I get, the less sense the world makes. Although from what my son says to me there aren't any Nazis up there."

"No Nazis?" Jack asked.

The old man shook his head. "My son tells me they're German prisoners but none of them are Nazis. The Nazis are sent to a different camp, he figures."

"But aren't all Germans Nazis?" I asked.

"That's what I thought myself, but my son was explaining it to me. The Nazis are people like Hitler

and his men. They're part of a political party, the
people who run the country. But most of the people
doing the actual fighting—the soldiers and sailors and
airmen—they're just regular sort of folk. My son says
they're fighting for their country, but they don't necessarily even believe in the things that Hitler's saying
and doing."

"They're probably only saying that now that they've
been captured and they know the war's going against
them," Jack snapped.

"That's what I thought, too!" the old man crowed. "But
my son told me that most of the prisoners are okay sort
of fellas. 'Course some of them are pretty important
fellas. Most of the prisoners are officers, including a
number of generals. They even have Hitler's favourite
U-boat captain in there—a guy who sank more Allied
ships than anybody else. His name's Kretschmer …
Captain Otto Kretschmer."

"Otto?" I asked. "We were talking to a prisoner named
Otto."

"Half the prisoners are called Otto, or Fritz or Karl or
Wolfgang. What sort of name is Wolfgang? So just how
was it that you boys were talking to anybody?" the old
man asked.

"We weren't really talking to him," Jack said, stepping
in. "We were walking by and this guy said a few words to
us through the fence."

"He seemed friendly and his English was really good," I added.

"Most of them speak good English, I heard. A lot took English when they were kids in school, and since they got here they've been taking courses to learn to speak better. Personally, I think that's foolish. Do we really want 'em to speak better English so it's harder to find 'em when they escape?"

"Have there been escapes?" I asked.

The old man paused. "I shouldn't be talking about any of this," he said in a low voice, "'cause it's all pretty hush-hush secret sort of stuff ... but even an old man who's half deaf still hears things."

"Things like what?" I asked in a whisper.

"Like the guy who got smuggled out in a laundry truck. And another who made himself a uniform to look like a Canadian soldier and just sashayed out through the front gate."

"And they got away?" I gasped.

"Not far and not for long. Both captured almost right away. The guy in the laundry truck gave himself up 'cause he was afraid he was going to suffocate underneath all that laundry! Can you imagine the look on that truck driver's face when a German prisoner pops up from the back and offers to surrender!" The old man started cackling. "Poor fella's lucky he didn't put the truck off the road and kill 'em both!"

The front door pinged and we turned around to look. There was a woman pushing a baby carriage, struggling to get through. I rushed over and held the door for her.

"Thank you," she said as she pushed the carriage into the store.

"We have to get going," Jack said to the old man.

"Come on back any time!" the old man called out. "And remember to tell your mother there's no better place in town for her to be getting her dry goods!"

CHAPTER FIVE

A FEW DAYS LATER we were back on the road out of Bowmanville, walking east toward Camp 30.

"Do you really think we should be doing this?" I asked.

"What's wrong with us going to see our mother and joining her for lunch?"

"This isn't about seeing Mom or eating lunch with her," I said. "We're going because you want to look at the camp again."

"And there's nothing wrong with that either. Besides, don't you want to see it too?"

"I do, but it isn't *my* curiosity about Camp X that almost got us killed."

"The key word is *almost*. We're alive, so stop worrying. Besides, what could go wrong here?"

I didn't answer, although I'd certainly thought about it. I never had trouble imagining what might go wrong. An escaped prisoner could take our mother hostage, or a guard might shoot one of us by accident, or one of the prisoners might shoot us on purpose! And I was sure there were lots of other possibilities that I hadn't even thought of—*yet*.

The camp came into view in the distance. My eye followed the fence, first in one direction and then the other. It was really big. This time I could see lots of activity behind the wire. Men were moving about the grounds, walking between the buildings or just standing around in groups. There were three men in a clearing passing a soccer ball while others, hoes in hand, were tending a flower bed.

"Probably too early for a game," I commented.

Jack shook his head. "Can't believe they let them play sports. That makes about as much sense as giving them beer and fresh fruit and vegetables. That old man at the store has to be wrong."

"I don't know. His son works here."

"And who gives a bunch of old men guns and tells them to guard prisoners? Shouldn't they have regular soldiers taking care of something like this?"

"You know we need all the regular soldiers fighting the war—they've got a more important job."

Jack nodded his head in agreement. That was something that had been happening more lately—Jack agreeing with me. Maybe after all the life-and-death things that happened at Camp X—breaking in, being captured and tied up and interrogated by Nazi agents, almost being shot to death, stealing the jeep and finally charging in to help save the day—he had more respect for me. I was still his little brother, but I wasn't his completely *stupid* little brother.

This time we made a point of staying on the road and well away from the fence. There were lots of prisoners around and we didn't want to talk to any of them. Maybe they were Nazis and maybe they weren't. Either way, they were the enemy, people who might have tried to kill our father.

Up ahead, across the road, we spotted the administration buildings. They were small, low, wooden structures—different from the big, brick buildings inside the fence. They looked as though they'd been newly built. We stopped in front of the first one.

"Do you think this could be where Mom works?" I asked.

"Only one way to find out." Jack started up the path and I followed. He hesitated for just a second before pushing in through the front door.

"Hello?" he called out tentatively.

There was a desk sitting directly in front of the door but nobody was sitting at it. In the background, coming from another room, I heard the noise of a typewriter and a phone ringing.

"Somebody's here," I said.

The words had no sooner come out of my mouth than a woman walked into the room. "Can I help you boys?"

"Yes. We're looking for our mother——Betty Braun."

"You're Betty's boys!" she exclaimed. "Come this way."

We followed as she retreated out of the room and down a corridor.

"Guess who I've got?" she asked as we entered another room. Our mother was sitting behind a big desk.

"Jack! George! What a pleasant surprise..." Her expression suddenly changed from happy to concerned. "Is everything all right?"

"Everything is fine! Honest!" I assured her.

"We just came up to say hello and it's almost lunchtime, and we thought we could eat with you," Jack said, holding up the paper bag we'd packed our lunches in.

"That is so sweet," she said, "but I'm going to be eating lunch with Colonel Armstrong ... inside the camp."

"What?" I gasped.

"You're joking, right?" Jack asked.

"Best food around," the woman who had guided us in said. "I wish I had time to join you today but there are reports due that I have to complete. Could you bring me back a sliver of dessert?"

"I certainly can, Doris."

"But I don't understand," I protested. "You're going into camp to eat with all of those prisoners?"

"It's perfectly safe," Doris said.

"Are you bringing in guards?" Jack asked.

"Just Colonel Armstrong," our mother said.

"Will he have a gun?" I asked.

"No guns are ever brought into the camp compound," Doris said.

"But that can't be safe!" I protested. "You're going into the camp without guards and without even a gun!" Even grandfather guards with guns were better than no grandfathers and no guns. This couldn't be right.

"Don't worry, it's perfectly safe. Ask the colonel yourself if you don't believe me," Doris said, gesturing behind us.

I turned around. A large man in uniform had just entered the room. Two soldiers jumped up from their desks and saluted. He returned their salutes as he strode across the room, the heels of his boots making a loud staccato sound against the wooden floors.

"I see we have some guests," he said. He was tall, had a neatly trimmed moustache and stood ramrod stiff. He was nobody's grandfather.

"These are my sons. Jack is my oldest, and my youngest, George."

He stuck out his hand and we shook. His hand was big and rough and he gripped mine firmly.

"The boys were just worried about their mother having lunch inside the camp," Doris said. I wished she'd just stayed quiet.

"It is perfectly safe," he said reassuringly. "I imagine you two must be here today because you're curious about what goes on."

"We just came to have lunch with our mother," I lied. "We thought we'd surprise her." At least that part was true.

"And maybe you also came to just make sure things were safe, what with her working so close to so many dangerous German prisoners of war," he continued.

"Maybe a little," Jack admitted.

"Then perhaps I can satisfy all possible concerns," the colonel said. "You'll see that she's safe, find out more about the camp and even have lunch with your mother."

Doris looked at the colonel and smiled. "You don't mean ..."

He smiled back. "Certainly. Would you boys care to join your mother and me for lunch in the prisoners' dining room?"

"I don't think that's such a good idea!" our mother said, jumping in before either of us had a chance to answer.

"Why not?" Colonel Armstrong asked. "It really is perfectly safe, and I think rather than telling your boys that, it would be far, far better to *show* them. People are more likely to believe what they see than what they are merely told."

"Please, Mom?" Jack asked.

I wasn't so sure I wanted to go there. Sharing a meal with Mom on this side of the fence was one thing, but actually going inside the camp ...

"If it's safe for you, it should be safe for us," Jack argued.

"He has a point there," Colonel Armstrong said.

Our mother looked trapped. It was obvious that she really didn't want us to come inside, but she didn't have any choice. If she didn't bring us now, we really would be worried.

"Fine," she said, with the tone of voice that I knew meant it wasn't really *fine,* but it was going to happen anyway.

CHAPTER SIX

THE FIRST GATE OPENED slowly, folding inward, allowing us inside. The two guards—one of them had to be sixty if he was a day—saluted smartly, and Colonel Armstrong returned the salutes. The guards all wore the same olive-green uniform, with a fierce-looking lion patch on the shoulder.

"As you can see, there are two fences, with a gap of fifteen feet between them. Both fences are twelve feet high and are topped by a rather nasty array of both barbed wire and razor wire," Colonel Armstrong said. "Along the outer fence at intervals of four yards are electric lights capable of turning night into day at the flick of a switch."

As the first gate closed behind us, the second began to open. The three others started into the yard, but I hesitated. Was this really wise?

Colonel Armstrong looked back. "Nothing to fear, lad," he said, and I hurried after them.

"As we travel, we are being observed from the guard towers. Each tower is twenty-two feet high and is manned by three guards equipped with rifles. There is not a spot within the fourteen-acre compound that is not visible from one of the nine towers."

That was reassuring, until I remembered that some of those guards were so old that they probably couldn't see very far anyway, and I didn't even want to think about how well they could shoot.

Colonel Armstrong turned around to face the guards. "Aren't you gentlemen forgetting something?" he demanded.

Nobody answered.

"No one asked us to sign in," Colonel Armstrong said firmly.

"Oh, yeah, sorry, sir," one of the guards stammered. He opened up a wooden box and pulled out a large leather book. "I'll mark the four of you in," he said.

The colonel started walking again, and we followed. "New regulation I've instituted to keep track of visitors in and out of the compound. The guards seem to have trouble remembering. I'm afraid it's hard to teach old dogs new tricks."

"I can't believe how old some of them are," Jack said.

"It's a reality of war that the younger men are on the front lines," Colonel Armstrong explained.

"Like our father," Jack said.

"Exactly. I have some fine men here, though. A bit long in the tooth, but many of them were good soldiers in their time."

"The grounds are very well maintained," my mother said, changing the subject. "The flowers are just lovely!"

"Yes, they are. The prisoners have established a horticultural club."

"A what?" I asked.

"A gardening club. They also have a theatre company, book club, poetry reading group, painting classes, a bird-watching club, a newspaper, an orchestra—"

"An orchestra?" my mother asked.

"Yes. Forty-eight pieces. They mainly play the classics, but the conductor has admitted a fondness for Glenn Miller and they've started playing some big band and swing standards. There are also many sporting events."

"Like soccer," Jack said.

"We saw them playing the other day," I added.

"And just what were you two doing up here the other day?" Colonel Armstrong asked.

"I sent them to see how long it would take to walk here," our mother explained.

"But we hung around for a while because we were curious," Jack confessed.

"Curiosity isn't necessarily a bad thing," Colonel Armstrong said. "Although I remember something my mother always used to say: 'Curiosity killed the cat.'"

As we continued along the path, two soldiers—two *prisoners*—came toward us. They walked crisply, the heels of their shiny boots clicking against the concrete walkway. I felt scared. I slipped back slightly so that I was partially shielded and protected by Colonel Armstrong. I looked anxiously around for the nearest guard tower, but didn't see any guards peering out from it.

As the distance closed to a few feet, the two soldiers smartly saluted Colonel Armstrong and he returned the gesture.

"*Guten Tag,*" one of the soldiers said as he tipped his hat politely to my mother.

"*Es ist ein schoner Tag,*" she said.

The man skidded to a stop and spun around. "*Sprechen Sie Deutsch?*"

"*Ja, aber nur ein bisschen,*" my mother replied.

"Ah. A beautiful day, indeed," the soldier said in very precise English. "It is so wonderful to hear even a few words spoken in my language by a woman. It has been a long time."

"It's also been a long time since I spoke any German. I'm afraid my accent must be awful."

"It was like music to my ears."

"Perhaps introductions are in order," Colonel Armstrong said. "This is my new administrative assistant, Mrs. Braun, and her two sons."

"You are all German," the other prisoner said, nodding his head.

"We're Canadian!" Jack snapped, stepping forward.

"My apologies," the prisoner said, bowing slightly from the waist. "I meant no offence. I mean there is German heritage."

"On both my side of the family and my husband's," our mother said. "His family came to Canada more than seventy years ago. They worked a farm in an area of Ontario that was once known as Berlin, in honour of its many German settlers."

"Berlin? But we live near Waterloo," I said.

"That was the name Berlin was changed to during World War I. It was better to be named after a famous British victory than the capital of the country we were at war with."

"War changes many things," the first prisoner said. He spoke some more words in German, tipped his hat again and turned and walked away.

"*Auf Wiedersehen*," our mother said.

"What did he say to Mom there at the end?" I whispered to Jack.

"Don't you remember any of the German you were taught when you were a kid?"

"I was a lot younger than you when our grandparents died," I reminded him. Our mother's parents had lived with us for the last years of their lives and taught Jack and me some German. Jack couldn't really speak more than a few words, but he seemed to understand it pretty well. As for me, people had to speak really, really slowly for me to understand anything at all.

"I was unaware that you spoke German," Colonel Armstrong said to Mom.

"I'm afraid it's rather a limited, rudimentary German."

"It sounded very good to me. I also speak German," he said.

"Armstrong is hardly a German name."

"I studied German and French in school. I always loved languages, although it appears to have worked against me in this instance." He paused. "I think if it were not for my fluency in German I'd be serving elsewhere, perhaps even in the European theatre, rather than being in charge of a prisoner-of-war camp. But enough of my complaining. Let's resume the tour."

We continued along the path.

"Judging from the condition of the buildings, I assume that this property predates the war," my mother said to the colonel.

"By more than a decade. This was originally built in 1929 as a training school for delinquent boys. Young men who were runaways or in trouble with the law were brought here to be reformed, trained and educated to become productive members of society. It was converted to its present use when it became obvious that we needed more sites to house prisoners. The first P.O.W.s arrived here last fall."

Colonel Armstrong turned down the sidewalk leading to one of the buildings. He opened the door, and as I stepped inside I was hit with a wave of hot, steamy air. Voices echoed off the walls of the corridor that stretched out in front of us. Both Jack and I stopped just inside the door, and Colonel Armstrong took the lead again.

"The playing fields are popular, but I think this building gets the most use."

He pushed open another door, and as I walked through I stopped dead in my tracks. It was a swimming pool … an indoor swimming pool.

"There is often a water polo match going on—very rough game," Colonel Armstrong said. "This is one of the few heated, indoor swimming pools around. It has a deep end suitable for diving and, as you can see, lanes for races. In fact, the prisoners recently had a swim meet—they called it the Aquatic Olympic Games. They had all manner of races. Their teams were divided into three groups."

"Army, air force and navy?" I asked.

"Yes," he said, and he gave me a questioning look. "How did you know that?"

"I figured it was just like the soccer teams. One of the prisoners said something to us through the fence when we were watching the game."

"That's not allowed," the colonel said.

"I'm sorry, we didn't know."

"But my guards certainly should. Didn't they notice?"

"Almost right away," Jack said. "The man just said a few sentences to us before the guard noticed and he made us leave."

"Better late than never, I suppose."

"Did the navy team win the Olympics?" I asked. I was curious, but more to the point I wanted to change the subject.

"In a landslide ... or should I say a tidal wave?" Colonel Armstrong joked. "A couple of the army officers had been taking swimming lessons prior to the Olympics, but apparently the lessons hadn't gone very far."

At that instant, one of the men frolicking in the pool dived to the bottom, revealing a very white, very bare bottom! A second did the same, revealing his behind! The men in the pool weren't wearing bathing suits!

My mother gave a little gasp, then a giggle and turned and headed for the door. We hurried after her.

"My apologies!" Colonel Armstrong gushed. "I had no idea!"

"I'm sure you didn't."

"Believe me, they all had bathing suits on for the Olympics," he insisted.

Outside, the summer heat seemed almost cool in comparison to the steamy heat of the pool area.

The colonel looked at his watch. "It's almost time for the second lunch seating. Come."

We continued along the path. German prisoners, alone or in groups, seemed to be everywhere. Those that passed right by us invariably saluted. Some remained frozen-faced, but others smiled or waved or said a few words in passing—almost always in English.

"That building to our left houses the gymnasium. Fully equipped."

"And tennis courts, there are tennis courts," I said, pointing behind the gym building.

"Last winter the prisoners flooded the tennis courts and turned them into an ice rink. Some of them have really taken to hockey," Colonel Armstrong told us.

Up ahead there were prisoners streaming out through a big double door and down a set of stairs. They moved aside as we started to climb the stairs. Prisoners—all in German uniforms—saluted as we walked by.

We entered a large, open room filled with dozens of long wooden tables. Many of the seats were now empty, while others were still occupied by prisoners finishing lunch. The colonel led us to a table at the very front. Unlike the others, this one had a clean white tablecloth. There were only two men still eating at the table, which was large enough for ten. I realized that I knew one of them—the man from the fence.

"*Guten Tag,* gentlemen," Colonel Armstrong called out.

The men rose to their feet and bowed slightly from the waist. There was no exchange of salutes, and I got the feeling that they had risen more as a courtesy to my mother than because of the colonel's rank.

"I would like to introduce the commander of the compound. Field Marshal Schmidt, this is my new assistant, Mrs. Braun, and these are her two children, Jack and George."

He extended his hand and shook all of ours.

"And this is Captain Kretschmer."

"I have already had the pleasure of meeting the two young men," Kretschmer said.

"Through the fence," Jack added. "This is the man we talked to."

"Although," Captain Kretschmer continued, "we were not formally introduced. If I had known that you were bringing guests, I would have altered my schedule and eaten with the second shift. It is always of great pleasure to meet and have conversation with new people."

"Perhaps another day," Colonel Armstrong said.

"That would be a pleasure. Especially to share discussion with two young people. We are not often granted that opportunity."

"You have children ... is it three?" Colonel Armstrong asked.

Captain Kretschmer smiled, a sad smile. "Two boys and a girl. I have a recent picture of them and my wife in my room. It came in the mail."

"How long has it been since you saw your family?" my mother asked.

"Two years, eight months and seven days," he said. "A lifetime ago."

I couldn't help thinking how long it had been since we'd seen our father.

It had been almost two years since he'd left, and we'd sent him a new picture of us only a few weeks ago. Strange, I'd never even thought of Nazis having families, so I'd obviously never thought of them missing them.

"And speaking of mail, Colonel Armstrong, we were very distressed that there was no mail call yesterday."

"That was unfortunate. I'm most certain there will be mail today."

"Most certain? Which is to say not completely certain?" Captain Kretschmer asked.

"There are some things that remain beyond my control."

"Mail call is the highlight of our days," Captain Kretschmer said. "It is the only link we have with those we left behind ... the only way we have of knowing that they are well."

"I understand the importance," Colonel Armstrong said. "Perhaps we could meet later on today to discuss the matter further."

"I look forward to that discussion. And I hope to have an opportunity to have further conversation with our young guests at some time in the future. It would bring me a little closer to my boys," Captain Kretschmer said. "But for now I must vacate my seat to allow other officers the chance to dine. It was a pleasure," he said as he stood up. The field marshal, who hadn't said a word, bowed slightly and then left.

"I was wondering about your arm," the captain said, pointing to Jack's cast. "How did you injure it?"

"A car accident," Jack said. "The cast is coming off really soon though."

"Perhaps then you and your brother will come to play in our gymnasium. We have basketball, volleyball and other games. You boys are welcome to come and use our facilities ... if that meets with the colonel's approval."

"I see no reason why not," Colonel Armstrong said.

I could think of a few reasons—like more than six hundred German prisoners' worth of reasons.

"Good day." The captain bowed gracefully from the waist and then walked away, leaving the four of us sitting at the table.

"The first gentleman, Field Marshal Schmidt, is the highest-ranking officer in the camp," Colonel Armstrong explained. "In fact, he is one of the highest-ranking German officers captured in the war. And Captain Kretschmer is, without a doubt, the most decorated German who has been taken prisoner."

"He's in the navy, right?" I asked.

"Yes. He captained U-boat 99."

"I don't know why, but I think I've heard of that," Jack said.

"I'm sure that you have—possibly from the newsreels. With Captain Kretschmer at its helm, it sank more Allied ships than any other German submarine. They call him the Wolf of the North Atlantic. He was personally decorated by Hitler on two occasions and is reported to be his favourite commander."

"But he seems so nice," I said.

"He is very nice. An officer and a gentleman."

"But he's a Nazi!" Jack protested.

"Please," Colonel Armstrong hissed. "We try not to use such terms ... especially while we are sitting among more than six hundred German prisoners."

"Sorry," Jack said.

"In fact there are no Nazis housed in this compound."

That was what the old man in the store had told us, but I was still having trouble believing it.

"These are all military men, many of them career soldiers. They battled in the name of their country. They fought with integrity and honour. Many have, in private conversations, also voiced their disagreement with the tactics of the Nazi party and are offended by the actions of those in charge." He paused. "Of course, those things are said only in private and are not to be repeated.

Almost all have family remaining in Germany. To speak out against Hitler, or even hint at disagreement, would mean the death of those family members."

"How awful," my mother said.

"The most fanatic Nazis, members of the S.S., kill without thought. Old people, women, even children."

"It's hard to believe that there are people like that in this world," my mother said.

Jack looked over at me. Neither of us had any trouble believing it.

"Enough of this talk," Colonel Armstrong said. "Let's enjoy our lunch. Today it's pork roast, with gravy, potatoes and cabbage. Their cooks are very good, and I'm sure everybody will find the food to their liking."

"Could I ask you a question?" Jack said.

"Go on," Colonel Armstrong replied.

"I was just wondering about everything ... everything here. It's all so fancy. It just seems like they have nothing but the best. And they're our prisoners."

"It does seem a little odd," Colonel Armstrong agreed. "I wouldn't imagine that either of you boys—perhaps even your mother—is familiar with a document called the Geneva Convention."

The old shopkeeper had mentioned that too.

"I've heard of it," Jack said, "but I'm not really sure what it is."

Both my mother and I shook our heads.

"It's an agreement between the countries of the world governing how captured soldiers are to be treated."

"And they're supposed to be treated like this?" Jack asked in amazement.

"They are to be properly housed, fed, given medical attention, allowed contact with family through mail, interviewed by the Red Cross and not subjected to physical punishment or torture."

"And the Nazis agree to all this too?" Jack asked. "Are our prisoners in Germany treated like this?"

"Not up to these standards," Colonel Armstrong said, "but that is because we hold *higher* standards. We are fighting a war to uphold the principles of integrity, democracy, fairness and the rights of the individual. It would be hypocritical of us not to treat their prisoners in a manner we believe to be fair and just."

"I guess that makes sense," Jack agreed.

"And by treating their prisoners well, we hope to persuade them to make attempts at fair treatment for our men who have been captured."

I thought about our father once more—his being captured or killed was a fear we lived with constantly. We waited for his letters confirming his safety the way Captain Kretschmer and the prisoners here waited for mail from their loved ones. I wanted to go straight home and write to our dad.

"There is also one other motive for the conditions we provide here," Colonel Armstrong said quietly. "By providing for their needs, we hope to discourage these men from making any serious effort to escape. We hope they will be reasonably content to sit out the war here."

"But people *do* try to escape," I said. "We heard about the laundry truck."

"Is there anything you two haven't heard about?" He paused. "Escape attempts are inevitable. It is the duty of all prisoners of war to attempt to escape. Thus far no one has been successful. Yet, as sure as I'm sitting here, some prisoners will continue to try to fulfil their duty. And I will fulfil my duty by stopping them."

CHAPTER SEVEN

"DO YOU HEAR the phone?" I asked.

"I don't hear anything except you talking," my brother said.

We were lying on the grass in our new backyard, in the shade of a big maple tree. We'd been goofing off all day—Mom was at work, we'd left our paper route back in Whitby, and school wasn't due to start for a few weeks.

"There it is again," I said. "Don't you hear it?"

"I hear it. It's probably coming from somebody else's house."

"I don't think so," I said, sitting up and turning my head to better capture the sound.

"Who'd be calling us?" Jack asked. "Who even knows our phone number?"

"Could be a wrong number," I suggested.

"And if it's a wrong number, why would I want to answer it?"

"Maybe it's Mom," I said.

"Why would Mom be calling?" he asked.

"I don't know."

"Only one way to find out. You go and answer it because I'm not moving. And you'd better hurry or whoever it is will hang up."

I jumped to my feet, ran across the lawn and bounded in through the back door. The phone rang again—no doubt now it was ours. I raced across the kitchen and grabbed it mid-ring.

"Hello!" I practically yelled.

"Is that you, George?"

It was Mom. "It's me."

"You sound all out of breath."

"I am," I puffed. "I ran in from the backyard ..."

"I need you and your brother to do something."

"Sure," I said, although now I felt like kicking myself for answering the phone in the first place. What chore was she going to give me? We were pretty bored, but lying on the grass beat the heck out of having to cut it.

"I need you and your brother to go down to Main Street, to the post office."

"Is there something there from Dad?" I asked hopefully.

"Not that I know. I need you to bring some mail up to the camp. We'll call to give authorization for you to pick it up. Can you do that?"

"Of course. We can take our bikes."

"Good. And you'd better bring along your old newspaper bags. Do you know where they are?"

"I'm pretty sure. But why do we need them?"

"You're going to be getting all the mail for the prisoners."

"You want us to do that?" It wasn't the kind of chore I'd been expecting.

"We need you to. The person who was supposed to bring it up called in sick, and then one thing led to another and the mail was never picked up. It has to be up here as soon as possible, so I need you to hurry."

"We'll get there on the double."

"Come straight to my office—and remember, the sooner the better!"

We pedalled along the dirt road out of town as quickly as we could, weighed down with our bags. They were stuffed full with letters and packages, and the corners of some of the boxes were poking into my side. A couple of letters fluttered out of my bag and fell to the ground as we rode. I saw them out of the corner of my eye and skidded to a stop to retrieve them. It would be awful to lose somebody's mail—their connection to their family. What would it be like for Dad not to get one of our letters?

I was sure nothing else had dropped out ... *pretty* sure. I shifted the bag to the front. It was harder to ride with it slung around me that way, but it let me keep one eye on the road and the other on the mail.

"I thought we were supposed to hurry!" Jack called over his shoulder from ahead of me. The cast on his arm wasn't slowing him down at all. I just wished he had a cast on his mouth!

I dug down a little harder on the pedals. It wasn't that much farther now. I could see the outline of the first tower poking over a grove of trees in the distance.

As we approached, Jack came to a stop ahead of me. I skidded to a stop beside him and realized why he wasn't moving.

There was a lot of action within the compound. Men, hundreds of men, were milling around in the open courtyard between the buildings. It looked like every man in the whole camp had to be out there. What were they up to … what were they doing? Were they planning on charging the gates, trying some sort of mass breakout?

Then I was startled by a series of shrill whistles, and the men began to assemble. Quickly they created four long lines, each line segmented into groups of five prisoners.

"What are they doing?" I asked Jack.

"How should I know?"

We were in a hurry, but our curiosity was greater than our need for speed.

The inside pair of the two double gates at the entrance opened and four soldiers—four guards—entered the compound. They marched in stiff military fashion until they faced the assembled prisoners, who stood silently and stiffly at attention.

One of the guards began shouting names. As each name was read, a man's voice called back in answer from the ranks of the prisoners.

"They're taking roll call," Jack said, "seeing if all the prisoners are still present."

"But what's to stop somebody from calling back more than once?" I asked.

"Good question."

As we continued to watch the proceedings, we noticed that two of the guards were walking through the prisoners' ranks.

"I think they're counting them," Jack said. That certainly looked like what was going on as one guard moved a hand up and down as he passed each man in turn.

"We'd better get going," Jack said, and we started off again.

We circled the camp, and when we came to the administration buildings we popped our bikes onto their kickstands and hurried into the office. Doris greeted us at the door and shepherded us to our mother's desk. Colonel Armstrong was standing right beside her.

"Excellent!" he said. "That was almost perfect timing."

"We came as fast as we could," I said, not mentioning the stop to watch the roll call.

"Now if you could just go one step farther. Could you please take the mail to the front gates and pass it on? The prisoners are already assembled for roll call, and mail call takes place right after that."

"Sure, we can do that," I said.

"But don't you have to check it first?" Jack asked.

"Check it?" Colonel Armstrong asked.

"To make sure there aren't secret codes in the letters or guns hidden in the packages."

"That won't be necessary. All of this mail has already been thoroughly investigated, even before it arrived at the local post office," Colonel Armstrong explained. "Although I'm suitably impressed that you would think through that possibility."

"Thank you, sir," Jack said, standing a little straighter because of the compliment.

"We'll get it straight to the guards," I said.

We started off.

"Boys," Colonel Armstrong called, and we stopped and turned around. "Your mother was mentioning that you delivered papers in Whitby."

"It was Jack's route. I just helped," I said.

"Will you be looking for employment here?" he asked.

"I hadn't really thought about it," Jack said. "Do you know somebody who works at the newspaper?"

"I wasn't thinking about the newspaper. I was thinking about here."

"Here at the camp?" I asked.

"It would actually involve doing what you did today, delivering the mail."

"Sure, we could do that!" I exclaimed, and then I thought things through a little bit further. "At least we could do that until school starts."

"What time does your school day end?" Colonel Armstrong asked.

I didn't know. Jack shook his head and shrugged.

"I was speaking to one of our neighbours about that very thing," our mother said, "because I was wondering how long you'd be alone at home after school before I got back from work. I was asking if she'd mind poking her head in just to see if you two were okay."

"We don't need to be babysat!" I protested.

"I wasn't suggesting a babysitter, just a friendly neighbour keeping an eye open and—"

"We don't need that either," I said. "Jack is old enough and smart enough to take care of us."

"That's so nice of you to say that about your brother. Regardless, getting back to the original question, she said that school ends at three o'clock."

"So if we went straight to the post office from school and then right here, we could arrive by three-thirty or three-forty at the latest," I said.

"So are you boys interested?"

"Really interested," Jack said.

"And until school starts, I might even have some other odd jobs you two can do. Nothing too important or fancy, but there are always things that need to be done."

"We'll do anything you want us to do," I said.

"Excellent. So your first assignment is to get back to your original task and take the mail over so it can be distributed to the prisoners."

"Yes, sir," I said. I had to fight the urge to give him a salute.

Jack and I left the building and hurried down the driveway and across the dirt road to the gate. There were two ancient-looking guards standing at the first gate and two more manning the inner gate.

"We've got the mail," Jack said.

"Colonel Armstrong told us to bring it," I added.

"Whatever the colonel wants. Go in," one of the guards said, and the second one started to open the gate.

"Go in? But I thought we were supposed to just—"

"He didn't tell us *where* we were supposed to take it ... when we get inside," Jack said, cutting me off with his words and a quick elbow in the side. Why had he done that, and what did he mean, *inside*? We were just supposed to bring the mail to the guards ... weren't we?

"See that big building in the centre, just beyond the parade grounds?"

I looked to where he was pointing. It was directly behind the assembled men.

"That's the place," he continued.

Jack and I slipped in through the first gate, which was now open.

"Jack, are you sure about this? Aren't we supposed to just take the mail to the guards?" I asked quietly so the guards couldn't hear.

"And the guards told us to take it in. Now shut up so you don't ruin everything," he hissed under his breath.

I heard the gate behind us close as the inner gate opened.

"You look a little scared," one of the guards at the second gate said, looking at me.

"He always looks that way," Jack said.

"Nothing to be ascared about," the second guard said. "Those prisoners aren't gonna bother you."

"And if they did, we'd be here," said the first, patting his rifle.

"Don't go scaring him any more than he already is," the second responded. "There's never been a need for anybody to fire a single shot at anybody. Proceed," he said, and we slipped in through the gate.

My first step into the compound sent a tingling up my spine. I knew from what everybody had said that we were safe, but it certainly didn't feel safe. Besides, what was Colonel Armstrong going to say when he found out what we'd done?

"Nobody had us sign in," Jack said. "These guys can't get anything right."

"And you think bringing the mail into the compound is right?" I challenged.

"We're just following orders," Jack said.

"What are you talking about? Colonel Armstrong didn't tell us to come in here."

"The *guard's* orders. He told us to bring the mail in."

"We shouldn't be doing this. We could get into big trouble," I said.

"How can we get into trouble by following orders? Besides, if we're wrong, it's an honest mistake. We were confused … we're just a couple of kids." He paused. "And didn't you want to come inside here too?"

I didn't answer because he was right. Part of me was excited to be here. But the other part was too worried to really enjoy the adventure completely.

"Wasn't the whole point of moving to Bowmanville to keep us away from Germans?"

"From German *spies*," Jack shot back. "These guys aren't spies. They aren't even Nazis. And it's not like it's dangerous. The colonel wouldn't have brought us here yesterday for lunch if it wasn't safe. You heard what the guard just said. There's nothing to be worried about."

I hardly bothered listening to him. My attention was captured by the lines of men, prisoners, German prisoners, stretched out before us. We slowly circled the parade grounds and listened as the roll continued to be called. Name after name—Lieutenant Krug … Lieutenant Konig … Captain Peterson—and after each name a voice yelled out in response.

The four guards conducting the roll call didn't seem to notice us. Most of the prisoners stood at attention, eyes straight ahead, oblivious. A few seemed to be following us with their eyes, and a couple turned their heads slightly to watch us as we passed. I guess the sight of two boys carrying newspaper bags must have been as strange to them as the sight of them was to us.

We went all the way around until we were directly behind the last line of prisoners. Everybody was facing forward, away from us. From back there I couldn't see the guards at the gate, so I assumed they couldn't see us either, which gave me a chill. I felt better when I looked around and realized I could see three different guard towers.

We walked up the front steps of the building the guard had pointed out to us. Jack pulled open one of the heavy wooden doors, holding it so I could walk in. It was cooler inside, and as the door shut behind us the sounds of roll call became muffled.

"Where do we go now?" I asked.

"How would I know?"

Jack moved slowly down the corridor. His footfalls echoed off the walls. I tried to make no sound as I trailed behind him.

"Nobody's here," Jack said. "But I guess that makes sense, because of roll call."

"So what do we do?"

"Wait."

The corridor emptied into a big room. Light streamed in through windows on the second level. There were empty desks, and doors leading off in a number of directions.

"Echo!" Jack yelled, and I jumped as his words bounced back at us off the walls.

"Why'd you do that?"

"Just for fun. It's not like anybody's around to hear——"

"*Wer ist da?*" called out a loud voice.

Jack and I exchanged startled looks, and a man——a big man with shiny black boots and a scowl on his face—— appeared at one of the doors.

"*Was tun Sie* ... what are you doing here?" he demanded angrily. "You have no right to be here!" he thundered as he strode toward us threateningly.

"We have the mail!" I exclaimed, digging into my bag and pulling out a handful of letters as proof.

"You should not be snooping around. You have no right!"

"We're not snooping. We're just bringing in the mail,"
I said.

"We're following orders, that's all," Jack said.

"Leave the mail and get out!" the prisoner snarled. He
grabbed the bag that was on Jack's shoulder.

"You get the mail, but you don't get the bag!" Jack shot
back, grabbing the bag, refusing to release it.

The prisoner looked surprised and stunned by Jack's
resistance. I was a bit shocked as well. Jack was big—for
a fourteen-year-old—but this man was much bigger and
stronger.

"You will give me the mail!" the man shouted, and I
jumped back.

"You can have the mail, but you can't have my bag. It's
mine and you can't have it!" Jack yelled back.

"Enough!" yelled a third voice, and I spun around. It
was Captain Kretschmer.

The prisoner released his grip on the bag and came to
attention, his eyes focused straight ahead.

Captain Kretschmer barked out something in German.

"Jawohl, Kapitän!" the prisoner called. Then he saluted,
spun around and marched out of the room at a double-
quick pace.

Captain Kretschmer came forward, looking at us, with
a questioning look on his face.

"We came with the mail," I explained in answer to
his unasked question. I held out the handful of letters

I was still clutching.

"And that goon tried to take my bag!" Jack added.

"What is a *goon*?" Captain Kretschmer asked. "I do not know that word."

"A goon is a big, strong—"

"He didn't mean anything by calling him that," I said, cutting Jack off before he could go any farther.

"It sounds like it is not a complimentary word," Captain Kretschmer said.

"He shouldn't have tried to take my bag!" Jack snapped.

"You looked as if you were prepared to fight him if necessary."

"Yeah, well, maybe I wouldn't have won, but he would have known he'd been in a fight," Jack said.

I half expected the captain to laugh, but he didn't even smile. He just nodded his head in agreement.

"You Canadians are nice people ... but not people to be angered. In a fight Canadian soldiers are known to be very brave, very tough ... not willing to give up even when badly outnumbered."

I could almost see Jack's chest puff out at the description. That also described my brother.

"We thought everybody was outside for roll call," I said.

"Everybody was, but they allow some of us, officers and those needed for administrative business, to be dismissed once we are accounted for. It is not correct for a field marshal to stand at attention in the hot sun. Now, if you would kindly leave the letters and parcels, I will make sure they are given out. The mail can be placed here on this desk."

Jack and I began emptying our bags onto the desk. A few letters flowed over the edge and fell to the floor. Captain Kretschmer bent down and grabbed them before I had a chance.

"We picked them up from the post office," I said. "We took good care of them because we know how important they are ... how important our letters from our father are."

"Obviously Colonel Armstrong has faith in you boys." He paused. "I think I also have faith."

I turned my bag inside out, making sure that no letters remained.

"Now, before you boys depart, could I interest you in a bowl of ice cream?"

"Ice cream?"

"Nothing too exotic. Only vanilla, but it is good ice cream."

"That would be—"

"We have to go," Jack said, cutting me off.

I wanted to say something to Jack because the ice cream really did sound good, but the serious look on his face warned me off.

"Perhaps another day," Captain Kretschmer said.

"That would be nice," I said.

"Come then, I'll walk with you two and we can talk. You could help me. My English ... I have some questions."

"Your English is great!" I said.

"It is improving, but I am only learning English from books. It is very formal. I was hoping to learn more words ... different words ... terms people use in daily living. Could you explain to me these terms?"

"What do you mean?" I asked.

"Things like ... like ... like ... *goon*. Tell me how you really meant it." Captain Kretschmer started to laugh, and Jack and I laughed along with him.

As we headed for the door, it opened and a number of prisoners came into the building. Roll call must have been completed. A prisoner held the door open for us and saluted the captain as we left.

"Would you like to see a picture of my family?" the captain asked.

Before we could even think to answer one way or the other, he pulled a picture from his shirt pocket and handed it to me.

"That is, of course, my wife, and these are my three children. The girl, she is the oldest, is named Bruna, and is sixteen. My boys, Wolfgang and Peter, are fourteen and eleven."

"That's sort of like us," I said, "except I'm twelve, but Jack is fourteen."

"I would have taken you both for older, at least a year or even two," he said.

I handed the picture to Jack for him to have a look.

"Canadians are big people," the captain said. "Good food, lots of exercise and fresh air. This is how life should be lived. Not in a prisoner-of-war camp, but in the open spaces."

"We used to live on a farm," I said. "Still would if our father hadn't joined the army."

"Ah, this war has changed many things for many people. Me, I would be teaching engineering at the university if not for the war. Teaching and returning each night to my wife and children, watching them grow up."

He stopped talking and I knew he was thinking about his family. It would be as hard for him not to see his kids as it must be for our dad—and as hard for those kids not to see him as it was for us.

"I never believed the war would go on this long," Captain Kretschmer said. "Four years." He shook his head. "I only pray it ends soon. My oldest son is not long from having to volunteer to fight."

"I'm going to enlist as soon as I turn sixteen," Jack said proudly.

"That would be unfortunate," the captain said.

"I'm not afraid," Jack said defiantly.

"Nor would be my son. Fear comes later. Those of us

who have been in battle know that fear is constant. You wear it like a coat, feel it with each breath."

"Our father's not afraid of anything," Jack said.

"And my son would say the same in my defence, but he would be wrong. Both your father and myself would be terribly afraid of one thing."

I waited for him to continue.

"My greatest fear was that I would not live to see my children again. And now, as the war pushes farther into Europe, I fear for their safety the way they had feared for mine. At least your father knows you are safe—that must be reassuring."

It was reassuring that neither of our parents knew how much danger we had already been in.

We stopped in front of the gate.

"Thanks for walking us here ... and for helping with that soldier," I said.

"You mean that big goon?" he asked, and smiled.

"Yeah, with the goon."

"It was my pleasure. Are you boys now going back to the administrative office?"

"Yeah. We're gonna wait until our mother gets off work so we can walk home with her," I said.

"I am sure she'll enjoy your company, as have I. I think I will go with you to speak to Colonel Armstrong."

"Go ... to his office, you mean?" I asked, feeling confused.

"Yes, his office."

"But you can't just go up and see him there, can you?" Jack asked.

"I know he is busy, so usually I make an appointment, but perhaps he has a moment to spare. He is usually very ... how do you say ... accommodating."

"But his office is outside—you can't just leave the camp," I said, feeling more confused by the minute.

"Well, yes, I can. Here, I'll show you."

CHAPTER EIGHT

"GOOD DAY, GENTLEMEN," Captain Kretschmer called to the guards at the gates.

"And a good day to you as well, Captain."

I'd never seen this guard before. Actually, I'd never seen any of them before. The four guards who had let us into the compound must have gone off duty and been replaced.

"Would you be so good as to open the gates?" the captain said. "I wish to go and see Colonel Armstrong."

"Sorry, sir, I'm afraid I can't do that," he replied.

I looked at Jack. Of course he couldn't do that. Prisoners can't just walk up to the fence and ask to leave.

"I can't open the gates until I know the identity of those two young men with you," the guard continued.

"What?" I gasped, unable to believe my ears.

"These boys are the sons of Colonel Armstrong's new assistant, Mrs. Braun," Captain Kretschmer explained.

"Are they?" the guard questioned. "When we came on duty there was no mention of them being inside the compound, and they weren't signed in."

"We ... came to deliver the mail," I stammered. "See?" I said, holding up my empty newspaper bag—which, of course, made no sense.

"I guess Herbie was so anxious to get home to his missus and a warm meal that he forgot to mention any of this to us."

"They came under the direction of Colonel Armstrong," the captain added. "You could call up to headquarters for confirmation."

"No need. If you say that's who they are, then that's good enough for me."

The second guard unlocked the gate and it started to swing open.

I stood stock-still. "You mean ... we can all go? *He* can just leave?" I asked, pointing at Captain Kretschmer.

"'Course he can. He always comes back." The guard turned to the captain. "You will return on your word of honour?"

"You have my word as an officer and a gentleman."

This wasn't real. I stumbled forward as the inner gate closed behind me and the outside gate began to open.

"I should not be any more than thirty minutes," he said to one of the guards manning the outer gate.

"Take your time, Captain. We're not going anywhere."

We all walked away from the compound—me, Jack and a prisoner!

"You seem surprised," Captain Kretschmer said with a grin.

"Well ... yeah ... a little," I stammered.

"Just a little?"

"A lot," Jack said. "It's kind of crazy that they just let you walk out."

"I must admit that it struck me as strange the first time," Captain Kretschmer agreed.

"So anybody can just go up and see the colonel any time they want?" Jack asked.

"That privilege would be limited to myself, the field marshal and some of the other high-ranking officers in the camp."

"I guess that makes sense," I agreed.

"But there are many other reasons that prisoners leave the camp," he added.

"Other reasons?"

"In the winter the cross-country ski team goes on outings. In the summer there are groups of men who go down to the lake to swim."

"The lake ... but Lake Ontario is miles and miles away," Jack said.

"It is a good walk. At a brisk pace it takes more than an hour. Then there is the group of men who go up to the farm every day."

"They go to a farm?" Now I'd heard everything!

"We raise most of our own vegetables and there are some fruit trees. Also goats and two cows."

Jack stopped at the door to the administration building. "So you're telling me that they just let prisoners walk out any time they want."

"There are some limits and restrictions."

"But what's to stop the prisoners from just leaving ... and not coming back?" Jack asked.

"Their honour. Each man gives his word of honour that he will return."

"And they do?" Jack asked in amazement.

"Every man has returned."

"We heard there have been escape attempts," I said.

"Yes, there have been a number of attempts."

"But you just said everybody came back." Now I was even more confused.

"Everybody who goes out, giving his word of honour, has always returned. Escape attempts are different."

"Like the guy who went out in the laundry truck, right?" I said.

"That was one attempt. Perhaps not the best thought out."

"But why do people even bother trying?" Jack asked. "There's no way anybody could make it back to Germany. It's impossible."

"Difficult, but not impossible. One man, Lieutenant Hans Krug, got across the border in the United States and then travelled throughout that country. He was apprehended in Texas—no more than one hundred yards from the Rio Grande. If he had been able to cross, he would have been in Mexico and free."

"That's amazing."

"And inspiring," Captain Kretschmer said.

"You know what I don't understand?" I said. "Why do people even try to escape? It seems like you're treated really good here."

"We are treated exceptionally good, but it is our duty to attempt to escape. To do less would be disloyal to our uniform and our country. Now come, I must speak to Colonel Armstrong."

We walked through the outer office. Doris gave us a wave and a smile—although I thought she was looking more at the captain than at us. We stopped at our mother's desk. She was on the phone, but she nodded.

"I understand," she said into the phone. "Supplies are limited for us all, but we have priority for building materials." She listened to a response we couldn't hear. "Good, I'll expect the truck here tomorrow. Thank you." She replaced the phone in its cradle.

"Good day, Mrs. Braun."

"*Guten Tag*," she replied.

"I was hoping that Colonel Armstrong might have a minute ... I apologize for not having made an appointment."

"I'll see if he's available." She reached over and pushed a button on a box on her desk. "Colonel Armstrong, Captain Kretschmer is here. He was hoping you might have a moment to see him."

"I'm rather busy," he replied, his voice tinny and detached, "but I will certainly put aside a few minutes. Send him in."

My mother looked up. "Please go in."

"Thank you," he said, bowing slightly and then turning to us. "And perhaps you boys would care to join me, since I am here to discuss you."

"Us?" I gulped. Were we in trouble? I knew we shouldn't have been in that building, and maybe we shouldn't have been in the compound to begin with, but we really hadn't done anything that was that wrong or—

"Do not look so worried, George," he said. "This is not bad. Come."

I looked over at our mother—she looked as confused and concerned as I felt.

The captain knocked on the door and then opened it. Jack and I followed him in.

"Good day, Colonel."

"And to you, Otto," he answered, his head bent over his papers. "What can I do for you on this fine—" He looked up and saw Jack and me and stopped. Now he looked confused too.

"I simply wanted to compliment you on your plan to

have these two fine young men deliver the mail."

"They helped us out in a tight pinch today and I offered them the job on an ongoing basis," Colonel Armstrong confirmed.

"Excellent. We are always greatly appreciative when there are fewer guards intruding in the compound, so it was good to have the boys bring the mail to our office building."

Colonel Armstrong's brow furrowed. "I had only intended them to take the mail to the gates and have one of my guards take it inside the compound. You boys weren't in the compound today, were you?"

I knew I was right, that we shouldn't have gone in. And now we were going to be in big trouble.

"We went to the gate and the guards told us the mail was supposed to go to the prisoners' offices," Jack explained. "We didn't know. We just thought we were doing what we were supposed to do."

"As did I," Captain Kretschmer said. "I did not know this was not intended. Nevertheless, would it be possible for them to take the mail inside in future?"

I expected Colonel Armstrong to bark out a no, but he didn't. He looked at Jack and then at me ... looked at us carefully, as if he was hoping to see the answer written on our faces.

"I will take your request under advisement," he finally answered.

"Thank you for your consideration," Captain Kretschmer said. "I do not wish to take up any more of your time." He saluted and Colonel Armstrong returned the salute.

"Boys," Colonel Armstrong said, "could you remain?"

The captain left, closing the door behind him. Colonel Armstrong stood up and circled around his desk. He sat down on the very edge.

"So you boys were in the compound again today."

"I'm sorry, we didn't mean to do anything wrong," I said.

"We thought we were supposed to go in to deliver the mail," Jack added.

"I'm sure you did. Did you feel comfortable being in there?" Colonel Armstrong asked.

"I was nervous ... at first," I admitted.

"And what do you think about Otto ... Captain Kretschmer's request? Would you be willing to go into the compound every day?"

"Sure, no problem," Jack said quickly.

"George?" he asked.

"I'm okay with it too ... if that's what you want us to do."

"The prisoners like to minimize the number of times my guards enter the compound. Roll call happens three times a day—that's unavoidable. And they accept that a certain number of unscheduled patrols have to take place. Most of my guards are excellent, first-rate officers and gentlemen, but some others can lack a certain tact in dealing with the prisoners. If you would be willing to deliver the mail, it would eliminate a source of tension."

"We'd be more than willing to help," Jack said.

"There is one thing, though, that I have to have your word on. It is necessary that you not talk to people about what goes on here at the camp."

"We wouldn't talk to anybody about anything," Jack assured him.

"Do you want us to sign an oath under the Official Secrets Act, like our mother?" I asked.

"Generally that isn't requested with people your age, although I imagine it could happen in certain extreme situations."

Jack and I both knew about those situations. We'd signed the oath already because of our involvement in Camp X, but even telling him we'd signed the oath would probably be breaking it. We couldn't admit our involvement at the camp, although I wondered if Colonel Armstrong already knew, and that was part of the reason he'd agreed to hire our mother in the first place. It was sure hard to know who knew what in wartime.

"You won't come across any secrets here," he continued. "But there's always a lot of talk, especially in a place as small as Bowmanville, and some of the locals are upset that the prisoners are given certain rights and privileges."

"Like the food they get to eat," I said.

He nodded his head. "That's exactly the type of thing. It sounds as though you've already heard some of that talk."

"We heard, but we didn't say anything. We just listened. We'd *never* say anything," Jack said. "You can count on us."

"I haven't known you boys very long, but I believe I *can* count on you. And knowing your mother, I feel certain you two are cut from stout cloth," he said.

"Stout cloth?" I asked, looking down at my shirt in confusion.

"It means you are strong ... solid ... reliable. The job is yours if you want it."

"We do, sir," Jack said, "and we won't let you down."

CHAPTER NINE

THE TRUCK ROARED BY, leaving us on our bikes in the choking, swirling grit it kicked up on the road. I closed my mouth completely and my eyes partly as I turned my head to the side and pushed into the cloud of dust.

"What the——?" I skidded to a stop as I practically rammed into the back of Jack's bike.

"Why did you stop?" I demanded.

"Because he stopped." Jack pointed up the road. Through the cloud I could see that the truck had pulled off to the side of the road. The wind blew the dust trail off the road, into the field, and it faded away.

"It could be anybody and anything," Jack said, reading my mind.

"Then why did we stop?"

"Because it could be *anybody* and *anything*. Weren't you listening?"

"What do we do then?" I asked.

"We have three choices. Go back, wait here or just ride past it ... on the far side of the road."

"And which of those three are we going to do?"

"I'm thinking, so I guess we'll be doing the waiting part. Look before you leap."

This was our third day delivering the mail. Yesterday had gone pretty smoothly. We knew where to pick up the mail, the guards knew we were coming, we went straight to the place where we were to drop it off, and all the prisoners were friendly to us—nobody yelled, like that first day. We even had another nice conversation with Captain Kretschmer. He did seem like a good guy, and he invited us for ice cream again. But we turned him down again. Actually, Jack turned him down. I was really ready for some ice cream.

"How long do we wait?" I asked.

Almost in answer the passenger door opened and someone stepped out.

"It's Bill!" I practically yelled.

He waved his hand, motioning for us to come. We raced our bikes over to the truck and skidded to a stop once again.

"You two planning on making me wait all day?" he asked.

"We were just being cautious," Jack said.

"Cautious?" Bill asked, pretending to look surprised.

"*Cautious* isn't a word I'd normally use when describing either of you two."

"We didn't know it was you. This isn't the truck you were driving the last time we saw you ... or the time before that, or the time before that," I said. "Do you ever drive in the same vehicle twice?"

"Sometimes twice, but not much more. All part of the game. People don't notice other people as much as they notice what they're driving. And I needed to talk to you boys about your new part-time jobs." He tugged at the strap of my newspaper bag, which was filled with letters and packages.

"How do you know about our jobs?" I asked.

He smiled. "We know everything. You must have figured *that* out by now. Well ... except for one thing."

"What's that?" I asked.

"We don't know what possessed the two of you to take a job that puts you in daily contact with hundreds of German prisoners."

"We were asked to deliver the mail up to the camp, and then one thing just sort of led to another," Jack explained.

"And somehow that led to you boys going right inside the compound. Judging by the way you kept sneaking into Camp X, I suppose you have no idea whatsoever what fences are designed to do. I'll explain it. Fences, especially those that are twelve feet tall and topped with barbed wire, are designed—"

"To keep prisoners in," Jack interrupted.

"And to keep other people *out*. Do you remember why we went to all the trouble to relocate your family in the first place?" Bill really didn't sound happy.

"Yeah," Jack mumbled.

"We needed to get you away from possible contact with Nazis. And now here you are, associating with hundreds and hundreds of German soldiers."

"But they're not Nazis," I tried to explain. "At least, that's what everybody tells us."

"They're not. And they're certainly not spies, they're soldiers. But that doesn't mean they're not in contact with Nazi spies."

"But how?" I asked.

Bill didn't answer immediately. "I'm afraid that is something I'm not at liberty to discuss."

"But if you didn't want us here, why did you get our mother a job at the camp?" Jack asked. I had to admit, that was a good question.

"That's the key," Bill said. "We got your *mother* a job. You two are supposed to be playing baseball, or swimming at the lake, or getting to know kids in the neighbourhood. And if you did want a job, why couldn't it be delivering papers—you have experience, you know—or cutting your neighbours' lawns?"

"We didn't know we were doing anything wrong," I said apologetically. "We're sorry, really sorry."

Bill let out a big sigh. "I guess it's my own fault. I should never have approved any plan that put you two anywhere near another sensitive military site. Both of you are too brave to be smart."

There was no way the brave part applied to me. Actually, the smart part didn't really fit either. I was just curious, and I let Jack lead me to places—and ideas—I knew were wrong.

"I guess another week or so won't matter much," Bill said. "Summer will end and then you'll be back in school and—"

"We were going to keep delivering the mail," I said.

"But you'll be in school."

"We worked it out. If we leave as soon as the bell rings, go straight to the post office and bike straight over here, then we can do it," I explained.

Bill shook his head slowly. He didn't look pleased. "A few weeks wouldn't have been good, but it would have been acceptable. Anything longer isn't. You boys will either have to quit or—"

"If we just quit, Mom will want to know why," Jack said.

"Then I guess you'll have to make it somebody else's decision. You'll have to get fired."

"Get fired!" I exclaimed.

"If you misbehave at school the teachers will give you detentions, and then you won't be able to pick up the mail on time. Do that a few times and the colonel will have no choice but to find somebody else to do the job."

"We can't do that!" I protested.

"Sure you can. Shoot some spitballs at somebody, dip little Suzie's pigtails into the inkwell, don't do your homework. It'll be easy—might even be a bit of fun."

"You don't understand," I said. "If we do that, our mother will kill us."

"It sounds like you're more afraid of your mother than you are of Nazi agents."

"You don't know our mother," Jack said.

Bill burst into laughter, and the tension that had been building just dissolved.

"Couldn't you talk to Colonel Armstrong and explain it to him?" I suggested.

"No can do. He doesn't know about your involvement with Camp X and he's not going to find out." Bill paused. "There is, however, one person I need to discuss this with."

I felt a rush of fear. He didn't mean our mother, did he? She'd been kept in the dark this long and I'd hoped that wouldn't change.

"I have to discuss this with Little Bill," he continued.

"Little Bill ... are you sure ... he's pretty busy, isn't he?" I asked.

"We wouldn't want to bother him," Jack said.

Bill was important. But Little Bill was really, *really* important. Too important to be bothered about the stupid kind of trouble we kept getting into.

"For some reason, he has continued to take a very personal interest in your welfare," Bill explained. "Now, you two had better get going before you're fired today. Say, that might not be a bad idea ... No, on second thought, just continue doing your job until you hear from me again."

That was a relief. "I have a question," I said. "I was just wondering—if you can tell us—how you knew about us getting this job."

"I told you. We know everything."

"Please?" I begged.

"Can't you two figure it out?" he asked.

I turned to Jack. I certainly had no idea. Jack shook his head.

"Where do you think the mail you're carrying comes from?" Bill asked.

"From the prisoners' families ... from Germany," I said.

"That's where it starts off, but it makes a few stops between there and the prisoners at Camp 30."

"Like the post office," I said.

"Like the official censors," Jack added.

Bill smiled and nodded. "And where do you think those censors are?"

"Camp X?" I asked.

"That's right. All the mail is examined at Camp X before it gets to the prisoners," Bill said. "And one of my men who was dropping off the mail saw you two pick it up. Now, I want you to go ahead and do your job as if nothing happened. Can you do that?"

"Sure, of course," Jack said.

"Good. You'll hear from me." Bill opened the door of the truck and then stopped. "And until I do get in touch, keep your eyes and ears wide open."

CHAPTER TEN

"A LITTLE BIT LATE TODAY, ain't you, boys?" the guard asked.

"A couple of minutes, sir," I said.

"Let's 'ave none of that *sir* stuff. It's just Smitty, plain Smitty, 'kay?"

"Sure, Smitty," Jack said.

Smitty was one of the Veteran Guards of Canada— maybe the most veteran of the guards. We hadn't asked him his age but he had to be in his sixties at least, and he spoke with a thick English accent. He was actually harder to understand than some of the prisoners!

"Should we sign the registration book?" I asked, reminding him so he wouldn't get into trouble.

"Spoke to our sergeant major, I did, and 'e said because ya was coming in regular-like that you didn't need to. You're not gonna be long, is ya?"

"Not long. Just got to deliver the mail and get back out."

"Better 'urry. Roll call is just about over."

Smitty opened up the first gate and ordered the second to be unlocked as well. We scurried through and then squeezed past the inner gate before it had opened more than a foot.

We were barely in before the guards dismissed the prisoners assembled for roll call, and men started scattering in all directions. We took the path that led straight for the prisoners' office building ... straight through a throng of men still standing and milling around after being dismissed.

There was a dream-like quality to the whole scene. Hundreds of German soldiers and sailors and air force officers, all in uniform, speaking German, and we were in the middle of it. Stranger still was the way we were greeted—smiles, hellos (almost always in English), pats on the back, questions about who we had mail for ... as if we'd know.

We reached the stairs and a soldier at the top opened the door. With a deep bow, he invited us in. We took the steps two at a time and bounded into the building. Directly at the end of the corridor, behind his big desk, sat Hans, the prisoner responsible for distributing the mail. Actually, although we didn't know him very well, it was becoming clear that he was the person who actually ran the compound, and not the big officers who sat behind closed doors.

He looked up at us and then glanced down at his watch.

"Sorry we're late," I said.

"You can correct that tomorrow."

We unloaded the letters and parcels from our bags, and Hans began arranging them in neat, orderly piles. Order and punctuality were important to him.

He picked up one letter, turned it over and made a clucking sound with his tongue. The flap of the letter was open.

"The censors did not reseal this one properly," Hans pointed out.

"Censors?" I asked, trying my best to sound uninformed.

"All letters and parcels are examined by government officials to see if we are giving or getting secret information."

"What sort of secrets would you have to give?" Jack asked.

"If I told you, then they would not be secrets, now would they?" Hans said, and he began to laugh. "Other than the fact that we had liver for lunch on Wednesday, I am not too sure what secrets I have to give. Actually," he said, suddenly lowering his voice dramatically, "we are not *allowed* to write about our meals."

"The Canadian government won't let you talk about what you eat?" I asked.

"Not your censors. My commander ... the field marshal."

"Why wouldn't he let you talk about food?"

Hans looked around anxiously. "Maybe I should not be saying this to you."

"Who are we going to tell?" Jack asked.

"Well ... it is just that we eat so well here. He thought it would not be good for the morale of our families to know that prisoners in Canada eat better than civilians in Germany."

"You guys eat better than civilians in Canada," I pointed out.

"We do?" Hans asked.

"Sure. We have rations for things like sugar and eggs, and most people don't get the fresh fruit and vegetables I've seen here."

"Then ice cream must be equally difficult to come by," a voice chimed in from behind.

We turned around. It was Captain Kretschmer. Hans leaped up from his desk and saluted.

"Ice cream is hard to get," Jack admitted. "Especially chocolate."

"Chocolate is difficult, but I do have vanilla ... if that is of interest today?"

It was of interest to me. I could practically taste it, but I knew Jack was going to turn him down again.

"Ice cream would be nice," Jack said. I turned to him

in shock. "Don't you want ice cream?" he asked me.

"Yeah, sure, of course!"

"Excellent. Let me put my bag in my office and we will go to the kitchen." The captain was carrying a leather satchel. He took a few steps and then stopped and turned around. "Hans, I need to see you in my office."

"Yes, sir!" Hans jumped to his feet again. He looked worried, but then again, he always looked worried. He followed the captain into the room.

"I wonder if he's in trouble for talking to us," I said quietly.

"That wasn't what I was wondering about," Jack whispered. "I was wondering what's in that bag he's taking into his office."

"Probably papers or ... Jack, why do you want to know?"

"Just wondering, that's all," he said, and shrugged.

Jack being curious could not lead to anything good.

"I was wondering something myself," I said. "Why did you agree to go for ice cream this time?"

"Just following orders."

"Captain Kretschmer didn't order us, he just invited us."

"Not him ... Bill," Jack said, the last word just barely audible.

"Bill!" I exclaimed.

Jack reached out to poke me but I jumped away.

"Sorry." I stepped back so I'd be close enough to my brother to whisper. "What are you talking about?"

"Bill ordered us to keep our eyes and ears open, so that's what I'm doing."

"He didn't mean here," I objected.

"Why not here? He just said—"

"Now, are you young gentlemen ready for a big bowl of ice cream?" Captain Kretschmer asked as he walked out of his office. Hans trailed behind him, his head down.

"We sure are," Jack said.

The captain turned to Hans, who was now at his desk again, and barked out a couple of orders. Funny, when he was speaking English he sounded friendly, but when he spoke German he sounded formal, angry, even frightening.

"Let us go."

Rather than heading out through the front door, we went past Hans's desk and down another corridor. I felt uneasy. I looked over at Jack. His expression was calm, and I drew some comfort from that. If there was danger, he'd let me know—unless he was the one causing it. I had this vision of Jack excusing himself, going back, thinking up some reason to get into the captain's office and looking into that bag.

"Could I ask you a question, Captain?" I said to Captain Kretschmer as we exited through the back of the building.

"Of course, but please, *Captain* is such a formal title. You should call me Otto."

"Sure ... okay, I guess." I shot Jack a look. This guy was sure being chummy with a couple of kids. "I was just wondering, what was it like being on a submarine?"

"It was like many things. Sometimes very quiet and calm. Other times scary. I really do not like enclosed places. I feel trapped."

"But you were a submarine captain!" I exclaimed.

"That is what makes the fear so real. I do not suppose I will ever be on a submarine again."

"Never?" I asked.

He shook his head. "My time will be spent here until the war is over. And then, whether we win or lose, I doubt I shall—"

"You're going to lose," Jack said, cutting him off. I held my breath, waiting for his reaction.

"I believe," Captain Kretschmer began, "that the war is not going in our, how do you say, direction, but it is far from over ... unfortunately. My greatest fear is not that we shall lose the war but that I shall lose my son. He is like you, Jack, only two years away from being expected to fight. To not see him for these years has been difficult. To never see him again would be ... would be ... tragic."

I'd had those same thoughts about our father. Funny, we were safe here and it was our father who was in danger. With Captain Kretschmer—Otto—he was safe, and it was his family that was in danger.

"Could you boys please do me a great favour?"

"Sure," I said.

"I know you have your opinions—and I respect those opinions—but there are some within the camp who would not be so respectful. I think it would be wise simply to avoid this type of discussion about the war."

"I'm not afraid of anybody," Jack said defiantly.

"I know you are not, my young friend," the captain said, placing an arm around Jack's shoulder. "Do it simply as a favour to me ... if you could."

"I guess I could," Jack agreed.

As we passed by one of the residences—they were all identified by number, and this was House Four—we heard the sounds of an accordion being played. Rounding the corner, we saw a man, sitting on a stool, playing. He was playing a polka, and while he was loud he certainly wasn't very talented. I was surprised that nobody had come out and asked him to be quiet. I'd have hated to have him playing underneath my window.

We continued walking until we reached the mess hall. Rather than going in the front door we circled around to the back. The captain pulled open a door and we entered the kitchen directly. One wall was lined with big, black stoves, and on another I could see a shiny metal door—it looked like a walk-in freezer.

There were four men at a table in the middle of the room, laughing and talking and yelling as they took turns throwing down cards. They wore aprons, and two had on chef's hats as well.

Suddenly all four jumped up from the table, knocking over chairs, to come to attention. They all saluted Captain Kretschmer. Along with the cards I noticed a pile of money in the centre of the table.

"We were just playing cards for a minute, Captain, just for a minute," one of the men said.

"The meal is prepared, sir," another added.

"And what is tonight's meal?" the captain asked.

"Beef tartar, cheese, butter and milk, sir," the first soldier answered.

"Good. Good. *Wie Sie waren,*" he said, and the four men visibly relaxed. They grabbed their chairs and sat back down.

Jack leaned over. "He told them to go back to what they were doing," Jack whispered to me.

"I just came to get some ice cream for myself and my two young friends," the captain said.

"*Sicher, mein Kapitän.* I will get it immediately," one of the men said, and he started to get up again.

"*Nein, nein, nein,*" the captain told him as he reached over and put his hand on the man's shoulder, easing him back into his seat. "I certainly know where it is kept, unless it is now in the oven instead of the freezer. While

I get the ice cream, you gentlemen could perhaps explain to my friends what you are playing."

"*Jawohl,*" one of the men said as the captain walked away. "This game is called skat," he said. "Do you know it?"

"Never heard of it," Jack said.

"In Germany it is known to even the littlest of children."

"We're not in—"

"Could you explain it?" I said, cutting Jack off before he could say anything else.

"*Sicher* ... um, certainly. It is simple to learn."

"If it is so simple, how come you never win?" asked one of his companions, and the other two men laughed.

"I said it was simple to learn. To master is very difficult. Come, pull up seats and I will show you."

Jack and I grabbed two chairs, dragged them over and sat down beside the man.

"First, we must have manners. You are George and Jack."

"Yeah, how did you know?" I asked.

"There are not too many young boys wandering the camp. Who is George?"

"That's me," I said, holding up my hand slightly.

"Well, George, I am Wolfgang—my friends call me Wolfie—and these men are Karl, Peter and another Peter." Each man nodded his head as he was introduced.

"Skat is the national card game of Germany," Wolfie began. "It was invented in 1810 in the little town of

Altenburg, which is about twenty-five miles south of—"

"Are you giving them a history lesson or teaching cards?" Karl asked.

"Just giving some background. It is a game played by three players."

"But there are four of you here," I said.

"Only one of the Peters is playing this hand," Wolfie explained. "We do not use the whole deck, only the numbered cards up from seven—so, seven, eight, nine, ten, jack, queen, king and the ace."

"That's like euchre," Jack said, "except you use from nine up."

"I do not know that game," Wolfie said.

"I know it," Karl piped up. "It has many things that are the same. Both use trump cards, and the jacks are most important."

"*Ja, ja,* that is the same. How about if we play a hand and you watch?"

Peter gathered up the cards that were on the table. He shuffled and then began dealing, three cards to each player. He then put two cards face down in the middle, nestled among the money that was lying there. I did a quick count. There were three five-dollar bills and at least twice that many ones.

He then proceeded to deal again until each man was holding ten cards. The man to his left, Peter, said something in German—was it a number? Then Karl said something, then Wolfie. Around and around it went. Maybe it would have made more sense if they'd been speaking English.

Wolfie set down a card, the ace of hearts. Karl played a nine of hearts, and Peter put down a queen. Wolfie laughed and then took all three cards, stacking them in a little pile to his left. I wasn't exactly sure what had just happened, but it seemed to please Wolfie and displease the other two. Hand after hand they put down cards. Whatever player cleared the three cards away led off the next round.

"Wait a second ... this is starting to look familiar," I said, more to myself than to anybody else.

"Opa used to play this."

Wolfie looked over at Jack. "Opa? Your grandfather, was he German?"

"He was Canadian but he was born in Germany," I answered, in case Jack was tempted to say something rude.

"Good for him! Let's raise a glass to your grandfather!"

All four men at the table picked up their glasses, clinking them together, and then drank, emptying them. The Peter who wasn't playing grabbed a bottle and refilled the glasses for all four. My nostrils told me what they were drinking was alcohol of some sort, but the bottle was plain and not labelled.

They continued to play, down to the last three cards. Wolfie yelped in delight and jumped up from his chair. This time he didn't just grab the cards, he pulled all the money toward him and squealed with delight.

"My first win of the day!" he exclaimed. "All I needed was my good-luck charms to be here! You two have brought me good fortune! Here, here, both of you should take some of the pot!" He held out two one-dollar bills.

"We can't take your money," I said. "You won it, not us."

"But I would not have won it without the two of you being here. Please, please take it!"

Reluctantly, Jack reached out and took the bills.

"Now, you must stay while we play again," Wolfie said.

"I am afraid that is not possible." It was Captain Kretschmer. "They have too much ice cream to eat." He was carrying a tray with three bowls on it—three bowls brimming over with ice cream! "Come, boys."

He walked through a swinging door that took us out of the kitchen and into the main dining hall. He led us over to the head table, the only one set with a table-cloth, plates and utensils. He gestured for us to sit and then placed a bowl in front of each of us. He set the third bowl on the table and then sat down himself.

"You will have to excuse the cooks," he said.

"Excuse them? Why?"

"It is a little early to be drinking," he said. "The kitchen staff use peelings from vegetables and fruit to make alcohol."

"I didn't know you could do that," I said.

"Apparently it is not a difficult task. Colonel Armstrong has made orders against it, and the guards try to find the stills, but not always successfully."

I didn't want to talk about alcohol. I wanted to eat ice cream. "Can we dig in now?" I asked.

"Dig in? That is one of those things I do not understand. It means?"

"Eat. You know, dig our spoons into the ice cream," I said, picking up the spoon to demonstrate.

"Of course! Enjoy!"

I sank my spoon into the mound of ice cream, dug out a huge heap and stuffed it in my mouth. It tasted wonderful! We hadn't had ice cream since we'd left the farm. Mom used to make it for us with the milk from our own dairy cows. But now, with sugar rationed, it was a treat that was hard to come by. Spoonful after spoonful I shovelled into my face. Jack was doing the same, although I thought I was getting to the bottom of my bowl faster than he was. I picked up the bowl with one hand and scraped the last bit out, licking the spoon when I was done.

"That was really good," I said, realizing that the words were a little distorted by my frozen tongue.

"I enjoyed it too," Captain Kretschmer said.

"But you've hardly touched yours," I said. His bowl was still almost full.

"I enjoyed watching you two *dig* your ice cream. I thought about how much my children would love to have some." He paused. "Hans probably should not have discussed it, but he was telling the truth. Things are very limited for our families in Germany. Food is limited. Basic necessities of life are in short supply."

"That must be hard," I said.

"It is. Sometimes I feel guilty for all that we are given here. It is a gilded cage."

"Now I don't understand what *you* mean," I said.

"Gilded. It means fancy, ornate, pretty. We are in a jail where our needs are well met, but it is still a cage."

"Is that why people try to escape?" Jack asked.

"It is our duty to try."

"I guess you'd have a lot of trouble in a tunnel," Jack said.

"I do not understand," the captain said.

"If you don't like closed places, it would be hard for you to escape in a tunnel—that's how P.O.W.s try to escape sometimes," he explained. "That's how Allied prisoners escape from Nazi camps."

"I had not heard that. Tunnels … hmmm … maybe we should start digging tonight. If you gentlemen are finished with your spoons, perhaps we could use them." He smiled, and I started to chuckle.

"Or perhaps you would be interested in using your spoons for another bowl of ice cream. I think I could persuade our head cook to give up a little bit of the chocolate syrup he has that he doesn't know I know about."

"That would be great," I said.

"We'd better get going," Jack said, and he started to stand up.

I reached over and grabbed him by the arm. "Another couple of minutes aren't going to matter. Besides, I know you like chocolate syrup even more than I do."

Jack resisted for just a split second and then let me pull him back down to his seat.

"I guess we can stay a little longer," he said.

CHAPTER ELEVEN

I ROLLED OVER IN BED, awakened by the sound of a phone ringing. I sat up. It was bright, so it had to be morning, but I had no idea what time it was. The phone rang again. I jumped out of bed and ran along the hall, then down the stairs, taking them two or three at a time. I hit the bottom, almost tumbling over as my feet skidded for traction on the slippery wooden floors. The phone rang again as I raced into the kitchen and grabbed it.

"Hello!" I said, panting for breath.

"Good morning."

I knew the voice instantly. "Bill."

"Did I wake you up?"

"No ... well, yeah, you did."

"About time. Is your brother still sleeping?"

"I think so. What time is it?" I asked.

"It's after seven-thirty. Your mother just left for work."

"Then Jack is definitely still sleeping. He sleeps a lot these days," I said.

"Go and wake him up. You two have to be out and on the highway within fifteen minutes. You have an appointment."

"An appointment?"

"Yes. On the highway in fifteen minutes."

"Meeting who, and——?" Suddenly there was just a dial tone on the other end of the line. I dropped the phone into its cradle.

"Jack!" I screamed as I raced out of the kitchen. "Jack! Get up, Jack!"

"So we have an appointment, but you don't know with who, and it's out on the highway, but you're really not sure where on the highway ... right?" Jack asked.

"Yeah, that's about it."

Another car whooshed by us, causing a few little cinders to skip up into my face in the trailing breeze it created.

"And you didn't think that maybe you should have asked for a few more details?"

"I tried to but the phone went dead," I explained to him again. "If we keep walking, whoever it is will find us."

"But you do think it's Bill, right?" Jack asked.

"He was the one who called, but somehow I didn't get the feeling it was him we were going to be meeting. Either way, I'm more worried about what's going to be said than who's going to say it."

"I don't follow you."

"Are we going to be told we have to stop delivering the mail, and that we have to get ourselves fired to do that?" I explained.

"Mom wouldn't like that," Jack said. "But if that's the worst thing that happens, that's not so bad."

"That's not the worst thing," I said. Jack stopped walking and I turned around to face him. "I've been thinking about it."

"You think too much!" Jack snapped.

"Maybe it's just that you don't think enough," I countered.

"At least I think enough not to annoy somebody who might box my ears," he threatened as he balled his hands into fists.

"I was thinking that they might tell us we have to move again," I said in a hurry.

"What?"

"If we had to move the first time because of something we did that put us in danger, maybe we've done it again. Doesn't that make sense?"

Jack didn't answer. Not disagreeing was usually the closest he came to agreeing with me.

"I don't know," Jack said. "All we've really done is deliver the mail a few times."

"It's been almost two weeks," I said, "and lately we've been doing more than just delivering the mail."

Now, after delivering the mail, we always stayed behind for a while. Sometimes we went back to the kitchen for more ice cream and to watch the cooks play skat. They even let Jack play a couple of hands, and he won three dollars! The cooks said he was a natural.

Other times we watched men playing soccer on the field or basketball in the gym. We even wandered into the hall where they put on their plays—they were rehearsing something from Shakespeare.

No matter where we went or what we were doing, I knew what Jack was really up to. He was keeping his eyes and ears open. He was being a spy. I wasn't sure what secrets he thought the prisoners had, but he was caught up in the game of trying to find out.

"I think we'd better keep walking," Jack said. "We're probably too close to town for them to pick us up here."

Looking behind me, I could still see some houses on the outskirts, so I figured what Jack said was true. Up ahead, the road curved hard to the right and then was blocked from view by a grove of trees. If I were picking somebody up, that's where I'd do it.

No sooner had that thought formed in my head than a car pulled off the road directly in front of us. It had barely come to a stop when the back door opened and Bill jumped out.

"Hurry up!" he yelled.

We ran for the car.

"Get in!"

I jumped in and Jack barrelled in behind me, shoving me clear across the seat and into the door on the far side. Before I could react I heard the door slam and I was thrown against the back of the seat as the car took off and swung back onto the road.

"Both of you onto the floor," Bill ordered.

We both slipped off the seat.

Suddenly I felt all hot and a flush came over me. My stomach turned, a shiver went right up my spine and my heart began beating very fast ... why was it so hot and why couldn't I get any air into my lungs? I felt panicky, like something bad was going to happen or—

"George, are you all right?" Bill asked.

I looked up at him but couldn't seem to speak.

"You're as white as a sheet. You don't look well."

"I ... I don't feel very good."

"Come up here onto the seat, both of you," Bill said. "We're well out of town now."

I climbed onto the seat. "Can I roll down the window? I need some fresh air."

"Certainly."

I gulped down a deep lungful of the fresh air flowing in the window. It felt good. I took a second big breath and then another.

"Some people need to see where they're going or they get carsick like that," Bill said sympathetically.

"That isn't it," Jack told him. "It reminded him of being on the floor of somebody else's car."

"Mr. Krum," I said. "It was like being in Mr. Krum's car." Mr. Krum had kidnapped us at gunpoint and made us sit on the floor of his car the same way so we wouldn't be seen.

"I'm terribly sorry," Bill said. "I didn't mean to bring back bad memories. I'll have a truck take you back so you can sit inside and not be seen. By the way, I hope you boys have an hour or so to spare."

"What do you have to tell us that's going to take that long?" Jack asked.

"The conversation won't, but the drive will."

"Where are we going?" I asked.

"Camp X."

"Camp X!" I exclaimed. "Why are we going there?"

"Because Little Bill doesn't have the time to come running out this far."

"Little Bill wants to see us? Do you know what he wants to talk about?"

"I have an idea, but why don't I leave that up to him. How long before you have to be home?" Bill asked.

"We don't really have anything to do until we pick up and deliver the mail ... Will we still be able to deliver the mail?" I asked.

"That would be telling, now, wouldn't it?"

"Could I ask you another question?" I said.

"You can ask."

"It's about Little Bill. He's your boss ..."

"Is that the question?" Bill asked.

"No. I just wanted to know ... Krum and those other Nazi agents, they were after him—I know that. I just wanted to know ... how important is he really?"

"Very important. I can't tell you much, but I will say that he's not just my boss. He's *everybody's* boss."

"Everybody?"

Bill nodded. "He's an extremely busy man. As it is, I don't know when he has time to sleep."

"But he wants to see us?"

"As I've said before, you boys are important to him— you're important to all of us."

"I just feel bad for causing everybody all these problems. We can stay away from the camp if that's what he wants, if that's what everybody wants," I said.

"No point in talking to me about it. Talk to Little Bill."

The car slowed and turned off Highway 2 onto Thornton Road. I knew exactly where we were of course. The main entrance to the camp was just up ahead. Again the car slowed, and it turned down the lane leading to the camp. It travelled a few car lengths and then came to a complete stop.

Four soldiers, two from each side, all carrying rifles, approached the car. The driver rolled down his window while Bill did the same with the back passenger window.

"Good afternoon, gentlemen," Bill said.

"Afternoon," one of the soldiers said as he bent down and peered into the car. I recognized him. "I didn't think I'd be seeing either of these two again," he said, gesturing with his rifle. Obviously he recognized us, too.

"You'll notice that they are on your list of those who may be admitted," Bill said.

The other soldier pulled a pad out of his pocket, flipped it open and began running his finger down a page.

"Just making sure," said the first soldier. "We've had enough of these two getting in here when they're not supposed to. Makes us all look pretty silly."

"They're on the list," the second soldier said. "Please proceed."

Bill rolled up the window and the car started up the lane. We were once again on the grounds of Camp X. The very few people who even knew it was here thought it was just one of countless military bases that dotted the country. Jack and I knew better. We knew it was a special base, a place that wasn't training soldiers but operatives ... secret agents ... spies.

The lane passed between and beneath massive chestnut trees, which painted the car with deep shadows. Up ahead through the front windshield I saw the farmhouse, the place we were headed. We came to a stop directly in front of the old building. Without saying a word Bill got out. We followed him up onto the porch and through the door. He led us down the corridor, stopped at a closed office door and knocked.

"Come!" came the voice from the other side. Bill opened the door and ushered us in.

Little Bill was standing at the window, his back to us. I could see he was wearing a civilian suit, not a military uniform. As he turned around I tried to read his expression. It was like a blank canvas. Not angry, or sad, or surprised or even amused. Just blank. Not so much as a twitch of his moustache.

"Sit," he said, gesturing to the chairs in front of the desk. Again there was no emotion in his voice. I felt anxious, but I was calmed by the thought that he liked us—that's what Bill had said, right? Bill sat in the seat to the right, Jack in the middle, and I sat in the remaining seat. I wanted to pull it back a little bit to get a little farther away from the desk.

Little Bill sat down and immediately began sorting through some papers. Finally he looked up. I remembered right away what his stare was like: sharp and penetrating.

"As I understand it, from speaking to Bill and reading the report, you two have managed to get inside Camp 30 on a daily basis," he said.

"Yeah, but it's not like here," I said. "We're not breaking in or anything."

"That's good to hear. We did so hope you'd limit the number of highly sensitive military installations that you *have* managed to infiltrate covertly. Bill tells me that you have been hired to pick up the mail, take it to the compound and distribute it to the prisoners."

"We don't really distribute it," I said. "We just take it into their office building and give it to a guy named Hans."

"Hans Mueller."

"I don't know his last name," I said.

Little Bill tapped the sheet he was holding with the index finger of the other hand. "I do."

"We really didn't mean to cause everybody so much trouble," I blurted out. "We know you have more important things you should be doing, and you shouldn't be wasting your time dealing with us. If you want us to quit delivering the mail we will. We'll even get fired if you want us to."

"We had considered that as one option," Little Bill confirmed. "I had even wondered if it might be necessary to relocate your family again, but felt that was unwarranted ... at this time."

I went from worried to relieved to concerned, all in one sentence. "At this time" could only mean that there still was a chance we would have to move again.

"I imagine you are familiar with the character of the prisoners being held at Camp 30. They are among the most important prisoners captured in the war."

"Like Otto," I said. "I mean, Captain Kretschmer—he asked us to call him Otto," I explained. "He talks to us all the time, and he's taken us to the kitchen and given us ice cream."

"It sounds as though he's befriended you boys."

Suddenly I felt guilty. Was it wrong to have ice cream with a German prisoner? Was it like being a traitor to think he was nice and be friendly with him?

"He talks to us all the time," Jack said. "Mainly we just listen. We try to keep our eyes and ears open."

"Always a wise strategy. The captain is a prime example of the high-ranking prisoners in the camp. Do you know why these prisoners are being held in Canada?"

"So they can't escape," I said.

"To make it more difficult to escape," Little Bill corrected me. "There is always a possibility."

"Like that one guy who almost got to Mexico," Jack said.

"Hans Krug," Little Bill said. "I see you really are keeping your eyes and ears open. I should never be surprised by what you boys know. You are very adept operatives."

Little Bill took a sip from a teacup sitting on his desk. "For some time we have wanted to place an agent within the camp to monitor the prisoners' activities."

"To try to figure out if anybody's trying to escape?" Jack asked.

"Oh, we're certain they're trying to escape. That's not a question. The questions are *who* and *how* and *when*. The difficulty for us is devising a plan to put an agent into the camp. Obviously they are not going to discuss matters with the guards, and it isn't as though any outsiders have access to the compound."

"Except us," I said.

He smiled. "Do you remember the last time we talked?"

"The last time you talked to me was in my hospital room after the car crash," I replied.

"And do you remember the last thing I said to you, George?"

"Goodbye?" I asked hesitantly, and both Bill and Little Bill started laughing.

"I know," Jack said.

"But you weren't even in the room," I said.

"But you told me. I remember." He turned to Little Bill. "You said to remain ready because you might need us again."

Little Bill nodded his head.

CHAPTER TWELVE

"WE'RE READY!" Jack exclaimed as he jumped to his feet. "Tell us what you want us to do and we'll do it!"

"Right now I want you both to just sit and listen," Little Bill said.

Jack sat back down.

"First off, I need to know how you're both feeling. Are there any lasting consequences of the injuries you received?"

"Except for this arm," Jack said, holding up his cast, "everything is fine. And the cast is coming off really soon—I'll be as good as new."

"And you, George?"

"I got headaches for a while, but not any more."

"I'm pleased. Next, I need you boys to have all the information, to fully understand the nature of your assignment, before you volunteer your services."

"It doesn't matter," Jack said. "We'll do whatever you want."

"Hold on," I said. "*I* want to know what you want us to do. I want to know *everything* before I agree to *anything*."

"Don't be such a—"

"Jack," Little Bill said, cutting off my brother before he could finish his insult. "Please be aware that any operative worth his salt wants to know all available information before agreeing to any assignment."

Jack closed his mouth and looked down at his hands. I felt a bit sorry for him.

"It's the duty of all prisoners of war to attempt to escape," Little Bill said.

"Both Captain Kretschmer and Colonel Armstrong told us that," I said.

"Yet there have been no attempts within the last few months," Little Bill continued. "Do you know what that probably means?"

I shook my head.

"It means that maybe something really big is being planned," Jack suggested.

Little Bill nodded his head in agreement. "We fear that there is a major operation afoot—a mass breakout, perhaps employing a tunnel."

"At least Captain Kretschmer won't be escaping through a tunnel," I said.

"Why would you say that?" Bill asked.

"He told us he doesn't like being in confined spaces any more," I said. "You know, like a submarine or a tunnel."

"He said that?" Little Bill asked.

"The submarine part," Jack said, "but I asked about tunnels."

"And what did he answer?" It was one of the first times I'd seen Little Bill look surprised.

"He made a joke about digging out with the spoons we were using for our ice cream," I said.

"Do you think they're trying to tunnel out?" Jack asked.

"That's the most common means of mass escape," Little Bill confirmed. "All precautions are being taken to detect any tunnelling that is taking place."

"But you still think it might be happening?" I asked.

"Hitler would consider it a major propaganda victory if he could reclaim some of his commanders. We want you two boys to tell us what you see and hear."

"We could do more than that," Jack said. "Captain Kretschmer has this briefcase that he carries around sometimes, and I think if I could get into his office and have a look, then——"

"Actually that's the sort of thing I *don't* want you to do. Far too risky. Just watch and listen. Jack, *sprechen Sie Deutsch?*"

"I speak some German," Jack answered. "I understand more than I speak."

"Do any of the prisoners know that?" Little Bill asked.

"I don't think so," Jack said.

"Maybe Otto ... I mean, Captain Kretschmer," I said.

"But he asked you to call him Otto, right?"

I nodded.

"Then keep calling him that. The closer he feels to you boys the better." Little Bill paused. "Actually, he's going to try to get as close to you as possible, so he can get things from you."

"What sort of things?" Jack asked.

"It could be information."

"Information about what?"

"He'll be looking for details. It all might seem relatively harmless, but the information would benefit them if they did get past the fence. He might ask things like: Have you been to Toronto lately? How long did it take to get there? What roads did you travel?" He took another sip from his drink. "It could also be more than information. Perhaps they will request maps, or ticket stubs for the train to Toronto or—"

"We wouldn't say or give them anything," Jack said. "You can count on us."

"I wouldn't be discussing any of this with you boys if I didn't feel certain that I could count on you," Little Bill said.

It made me feel good to know he trusted us.

"But I'm actually counting on you to give him what he wants," Little Bill went on.

"I don't understand," I said.

"Me neither," Jack said. "You want us to *help* them escape?"

"Let me explain. If they request a map, then you report it to us. We will arrange for you to have a very special map. One that distorts distances, doesn't quite show where things really are, that will actually provide *mis*information instead."

"I understand. So whatever they want or whatever we're asked about, you want to know, so you can figure out what they might be up to," I said.

"Correct," Little Bill said. "But I also need you boys to be aware of the possible consequences of your role. If your mission is discovered, you could be in danger."

I didn't like the sound of that, but I was hardly surprised. What would the prisoners do to us if they found out what we were up to?

"If you're compromised, it might mean that we'll have to move your family once again," Little Bill said.

"I hope that doesn't happen," I admitted.

"It would be unfortunate, but if necessary we will pursue it. There's also one other thing you need to think about. The only people who know about your mission are myself and Bill. Nobody else—not Colonel Armstrong and obviously none of the guards—will be aware of your role."

"That's probably good," I said, thinking that the fewer people who knew the better.

"It could be very good or very bad," Little Bill said. "If the guards catch you passing on information or anything else to the prisoners, you will be seen as traitors."

"But ... but we'd only be doing what you told us to do," I stammered.

"You would be following my orders," Little Bill agreed. "But nobody would know that."

"But wouldn't you tell them then?" I asked. I couldn't believe we'd be left hanging out to dry.

"I'd arrange for you to be released and for your family to be relocated, but nobody would be aware of your true role. To the people of Bowmanville you'd be known as fools, or worse ... traitors and collaborators who offered comfort to the enemy."

"I don't care about other people," Jack said. "What would our mother know? Would she know the truth?"

"Just as we couldn't allow her to know that you boys were heroes at Camp X, we couldn't let her know of this. We couldn't reveal your true role without risking our security and other critical operations."

I was prepared for a lot of things. But I was not prepared to have our mother—and our father—think of us as traitors. I'd been faced with death. This seemed so much worse.

"They'd *never* know the truth?" I asked.

"Perhaps, after the war is over. But until then we would have to keep people in the dark."

"That would be awful … to have people think of us that way," I said forlornly.

"Yes. Sometimes the truth must be sacrificed," Little Bill said. "Now, I imagine you boys need time to consider all the factors before you make a decision. I would think nothing less of you if you chose to decline this assignment."

"No, we don't need to think about it," Jack said firmly.

"We don't?" I asked.

He shook his head. "First off, we're not going to get caught. And second, if this is what we need to do, if this is our assignment, we'll do it." Jack turned directly to me. "Do you think our father has any choice when he's sent into battle?"

I looked from Jack to Bill to Little Bill. "We're in," I said.

CHAPTER THIRTEEN

"GOOD AFTERNOON, HANS," I said as we walked up to his desk.

He looked up from the work spread out before him. He always seemed to be working.

"Good afternoon, boys. You are right here on the dot ... Is that right ... the dot? Does that mean on time?"

"It does, and we are," I said.

"Captain Kretschmer would like to speak to you."

"Is he in his office?" Jack asked. I knew Jack was dying to have a look in there.

"No. He is in the auditorium. "

"Where's that?" I asked.

"On the other side of the compound. Big building, two storeys tall."

"Okay, I know the one," Jack said. "That's where they were rehearsing a play."

Jack and I dumped our bags onto Hans's desk and the

mail flowed out. Some letters and parcels spilled over the sides, hitting the floor.

"Please ... please ... take more care!" Hans exclaimed as he leaped to his feet and tried to stop any more letters from falling.

We kept pouring until the bags were empty and his once-organized desk was a mass of unsorted, untidy mail. Hans bent down and scooped up the letters and parcels, clucking to himself and saying something in German under his breath. Even though I didn't understand the words I had a pretty good idea what they meant. He was never happy when things weren't organized and proper. I got the feeling that Jack actually enjoyed bothering Hans. Jack had said to me: "If the Germans are so precise and organized how come they're losing the war?"

"Do you know what he wants to talk to us about?" I asked Hans.

"*Nein, nein.* Commanders don't tell their inferiors what they wish to discuss."

"You're working on a need-to-know basis and you don't need to know anything," I joked.

Jack shot me a dirty look—what was wrong with me, kidding Hans?

"We have to get going," Jack said. "We don't want to keep Otto waiting."

"Otto," Hans echoed, shaking his head sadly. "Children

should never refer to an adult by his first name—it shows no respect."

"He asked us to call him Otto," I said.

"In Germany, children—"

"And we're not in Germany," Jack added.

Jack spun around and started off. I waved goodbye to a startled-looking Hans and caught up with my brother.

"You gotta learn to keep your mouth shut," Jack said.

"Me? I wasn't the one insulting Hans."

Jack stopped as we got outside the door, grabbed me by the front of my shirt and pulled me close to him. "And I'm not the one saying things like 'on a need-to-know basis.' Do you remember who said that to you?"

"Of course I do. It was one of the ..." I didn't complete the sentence. It was one of the guards at Camp X.

"You don't know what connections these guys might make that would betray us," he said, his voice barely a whisper. "Understand?"

"I understand. I'm sorry. I won't let it happen again."

"It better not."

"Could you let me go now?" I asked. "People are looking."

A couple of men passing by were craning their necks to watch us. Jack let go of my shirt and then brushed his hands down the front to straighten it.

"Let's go."

"But isn't the building we want that way?" I asked, pointing in almost the opposite direction from where he was heading.

"Just follow me," Jack said.

"But we could get there a lot faster if we——" Jack had continued walking. He was way ahead now and I was talking to myself.

"Did it ever occur to you that getting there faster isn't as important as having a chance to wander around and investigate?" Jack asked as I caught up to him again.

"Obviously not."

"Just keep your mouth shut and your eyes and ears open. You know that's why God gave you one mouth and two eyes and ears—you should look and listen twice as much as you talk. With you, it's the other way around."

We circled around the side of one of the residences and we were greeted, as usual, by the blaring of accordion music.

"Doesn't that guy ever get tired of playing?" I asked.

"Doesn't look like it, although I'm pretty tired of hearing it."

"Either he plays all the time or he saves his music for when we're around," I said.

"Nope," Jack replied. "I heard some of the guards talking about how they'd like him to quit too."

Continuing around the building and along the fence, we passed prisoners moving in the other direction, or simply standing, smoking, talking. There were two groups on the playing field. It looked as though they were warming up.

"Do you think we could stick around and watch some of the game?" I asked.

"Maybe we could stick around, but it wouldn't be to watch the game."

"Then what?"

"You know how popular those games are. Practically all the prisoners go and watch."

"Yeah, well, they're good games," I said.

"I was thinking that would be a pretty good time to be somewhere else on the compound. You know, just strolling around without anybody to see us."

"What do you mean by 'strolling'?" I asked.

"Just walking. Maybe looking in some of the buildings as we pass. Aren't you curious about what's going on here?"

"Curious I am. Stupid I'm not."

We finally came around to the back of the auditorium. We made our way up the steps to the front door and entered, and immediately became aware of loud voices. What was everyone yelling about?

Then we saw. There was a stage, and people were wearing costumes—old-fashioned costumes. They were working on their play, a dozen men and a woman. Where had the woman come from?

I could make out the words now—they weren't yelling, they were saying their lines loudly for an imaginary audience at the back of the hall. They were speaking English, but it sounded strange. Not just because of the German accents—some of the words were just funny ... old-fashioned, just like the costumes.

"Pssst!"

It was Otto. He was sitting on a bench along the back wall. We walked over and sat down beside him.

"Rehearsal," he whispered. "Dress rehearsal. The play is to be performed in two weeks."

"What play is it?" I whispered back.

"Romeo and Juliet."

"Is that Juliet?" I asked, pointing to the woman on stage. He nodded.

"Where did she come from? There aren't any women prisoners here ... are there?"

"Juliet is a prisoner, but *he* isn't a woman. Juliet is being played by an army officer named Karl Hirsch."

"That's a man?" Jack asked.

"Yes, but he makes a lovely woman."

"Why didn't you just pick a different play?" I asked.

"Almost all plays have at least one female in them," Otto explained.

"But *Romeo and Juliet*?" I questioned.

"It is a classic. Although we have had to change some of the scenes—Karl was agreeable to playing a woman, but not to kissing our Romeo. In truth, we are simply going back to Shakespeare's roots."

"I don't understand," I said.

"In the original days, when Shakespeare was writing and his plays were being performed, all the parts were played by males."

"All the parts? Even Juliet?"

"*Ja.* Our actors are very good. Do you boys wish to come to the performance?"

"Could we?" I asked.

"You would be my very special guests. Do you ever go to the theatre?"

"We went to a show last Christmas," I said.

"In Toronto," Jack added.

"Toronto?" Otto said. "I hear it is a very nice city."

"I don't know about nice, but it is big," Jack said.

"I hope to visit it someday ... after the war. It is not far from here, correct?"

"Not far," I said. This was too strange—it was happening just the way Little Bill had said it would!

"I am told that the main street of Bowmanville— Highway 2—leads right to Toronto."

"You could drive there in less than an hour if you had a car," I said.

"Quicker if you had a fast car," Jack added.

"It is hard for me to get it all in my head," Otto said. "I know we are near Bowmanville, but I am so curious about the towns and villages around here. Many of us wonder if we might come back to Canada someday, not only to visit but to settle. It would be most helpful to learn about the surrounding communities."

"It's easier if you can look at them on a map," Jack said.

I felt the hairs on the back of my neck bristle. I tried to not even blink.

"Do you have a map?" Jack asked.

"No."

"We've got a map at home. Would you like me to bring it in for you to see?"

"If it's no trouble, I would appreciate that."

"It would be no trouble at all," Jack said, cool as a cucumber.

"Do you think I could keep the map … you know … take it back to Germany with me when I go?" Otto said.

"I guess … It didn't cost that much," Jack said.

"Oh, I would pay you for it. I will give you five dollars."

"Five dollars!" I exclaimed. "It couldn't have cost more than fifty cents!"

"Or even less," Jack said.

"But it is worth more to me than that. Besides, what else do I have to spend my money on? Consider the extra money to be a delivery charge."

"You're on!" Jack said, I could tell his enthusiasm was all for show. "But I'm not exactly sure where the map is.

It might take me a couple of days to find it—some of our stuff is still in boxes after the move."

"I understand. A few days would be fine."

"We'd better get going now," Jack said. "We'll see you tomorrow."

Jack and I left the building. I started in one direction and Jack turned in the other. I quickly caught up with him.

"It was just like Little Bill said," I told Jack.

"Exactly. We have to contact Bill and have them get us a special map. I hope it won't take too long."

"Is that why you said you didn't know exactly where the map was?" I asked.

"I was buying time. Hey, look, there's the chair and the accordion but no accordion player," Jack said, pointing ahead toward House Four.

"I guess he finally got tired of playing."

The words had barely escaped my lips when the man came out of the building, saw us, and practically ran over and grabbed his instrument. He began playing before he'd even strapped it on—which made it sound even worse than before.

"That's strange," Jack said.

"With all the practice, you'd figure he'd be getting better."

"Yeah, you would."

Jack suddenly veered off the path so he was headed straight for the accordion player. What was he doing that for? We needed to get farther away from this guy, not closer.

"Hi!" Jack called over the strained chords.

The man nodded and gave a nervous little smile but he didn't stop playing.

"Nice accordion!" Jack called. "You play well!"

The man nodded his head again but didn't say anything. He just kept playing. He even got a little bit louder and, unbelievably, worse.

"Have you been playing for long?" Jack asked.

Why was Jack being so talkative? That just wasn't like him. The man kept on playing.

My attention was caught by movement just off to the left. A man walked out of the building, followed by a second man, and then two more, and two more after that. They turned to the left and quickly walked away. They seemed to be in a hurry. So much of a hurry, in fact, that nobody even looked our way. It was like they didn't notice us, and we were only ten feet from the door.

The accordion man suddenly stopped playing. He took the accordion off his chest and slung it over one shoulder.

"Time to dinner," he said in broken, heavily accented English. That must have been why he hadn't answered the questions—his English wasn't very good.

"Good bye-bye," he said, bowing from the waist, then turning and rushing off down the path to follow the others.

"What time is it?" Jack asked.

I looked at my watch. "Almost four-thirty."

"That's what I thought. First dinner serving isn't until six. So why was he rushing away?"

"Maybe he didn't know the time, or maybe he just wanted to catch up to his friends," I suggested.

"Friends? Those guys didn't even look in his direction. It was like they were working hard not to look at him, or us," Jack said. "Didn't you notice?"

"Now that you mention it."

"And did you notice anything about the accordion player?" Jack asked.

"Just that he seems to be getting worse."

"I don't care about how he's playing. I'm trying to figure out *why* he's playing."

"Maybe he just likes the accordion," I suggested.

"No," Jack said, shaking his head. "Something's going on in this building. I don't know what, but something."

"Yeah, so shouldn't we tell Bill? Isn't that what we're supposed to be doing?"

"I will—when I've got some real evidence. Right now I've got nothing but a hunch, and if I tell him that I'll just look like a jerk!"

"You're not going to suggest something stupid like going inside, are you?" I asked.

"Of course not." I felt relieved. "Not now. Too many people around. But I'll look for our chance."

I knew he would, and that made me even more nervous.

"Let's get out of here so nobody thinks we're suspicious," Jack said. "We gotta get home so we can contact Bill and tell him about the map."

CHAPTER FOURTEEN

JACK DROPPED HIS BAG onto the corner of Hans's desk, causing the coffee cup at the edge to shake precariously.

"Be careful!" Hans exclaimed as he grabbed his cup before it could spill.

"Sorry," I said, offering the apology that I knew Jack wasn't going to be giving.

Jack turned his bag inside out. I caught sight of the newspaper tumbling out with all the letters and parcels and tried to look elsewhere. I wasn't supposed to see it because it wasn't supposed to be there. It was something that Bill had given to us—along with the map that the captain had asked for a few days ago. Bill had asked us to slip the newspaper in the bag and pretend that somehow it had accidentally gotten in there without our knowing.

Prisoners weren't supposed to have newspapers, but this, of course, wasn't a real paper. It was identical to the regular *Toronto Daily Star* except for a few articles and a few pieces of information——or I guess pieces of misinformation——that had been inserted.

Bill didn't tell us what they'd changed, and we didn't ask. I could only imagine. It was amazing to think that they could change a newspaper like that, but the more I knew about this spy stuff, the more I realized there wasn't much they couldn't do.

Hans muttered as he tried to organize the mountain of mail. I started to add more letters from my bag when I noticed he'd stopped mumbling. I looked down at him and saw that he'd noticed the paper. He swept a bunch of letters over top to cover it up and I looked away.

"Is Otto around?" Jack asked.

"The *Kapitän* is in his office," Hans said. "Is he expecting you? Do you have an appointment?"

"No appointment, but he'll want to see us."

"I'll see if ... Just go and knock on his door," Hans offered.

I realized he didn't want to go and look himself because he was still trying to keep the paper hidden from our view.

We walked over to Otto's door and knocked.

"Kommen Sie!" came the voice through the closed door. He sounded official and angry.

"That means you can go in," Hans called from behind us.

The actual translation was simply "Come." I knew that. Jack and I had been having our mother teach us German words at night. She was so happy we wanted to learn the language. If she'd had any idea why, she wouldn't have been nearly so pleased. The more we understood, the better our chances of hearing something we were better off not knowing.

Jack opened the door. Otto was seated at his desk, papers strewn about. He looked up, smiled and motioned for us to enter.

"Good day, boys. I hope you have stopped in to invite me to take an ice cream break."

"We brought you something," Jack said. He pulled the folded road map out of his pocket.

Otto saw what it was and his expression brightened. "Please, sit ... Um, George, could you close the door first?"

I was only too happy to close the door. The last thing in the world I wanted was for anybody to see us handing over the map. It had been awful going through the gates, knowing what Jack was carrying. If the map had been discovered, Jack was going to tell the guards he'd just forgotten he had it, but I still felt nervous.

"Sorry it took so long," Jack said. "The map was at the bottom of the last box to be unpacked."

"Always the way," Otto said.

Of course the map hadn't been in any box. A whole

week passed before Bill got the map to us—it wasn't like they'd picked it up at a gas station. They'd altered the map in some small but important ways.

Otto took the map and unfolded it, spreading it across his desk.

I felt a wave of anxiety. The map looked like a regular Ontario road map. It even had a couple of rips along the folds, and one of the corners was tattered and torn to make it look as though the map could have been in a box in our house. It certainly looked real to me. The question was, would Otto think it was real?

As I sat there looking at him examining the map, I wondered what would happen if he found out what we were doing. I had this vision of him sitting bolt upright, telling us he knew this was a forged map and we wouldn't be leaving the compound alive.

"So we are right here," Otto said, touching the map at what I assumed was Bowmanville. I turned my head sideways to try to see the map more clearly.

"And just down the road is Toronto ... less than an hour away." He looked up. "Highway 2 is the best route, correct?"

"It goes from here to Whitby and then to Toronto," I said.

"Whitby?" he asked. "I know that place—that is where they send our laundry. Strange you should mention there."

I knew I'd made a mistake. I shouldn't have mentioned Whitby. But how could I get out of it now?

"We have an aunt who lives there," Jack said. "It's not much of anything, but we've been there before. Why would they send your laundry there?"

"That is a question I have asked myself," Otto said. He looked back down at the map. "This is such a vast country. Why, this Lake Ontario is almost as big as the entire country of Germany. It is like an inland sea. Can you imagine the havoc it would cause if a German submarine could penetrate this far? But of course that is not possible." He tapped his finger against the map. "There are rapids ... here ... here ... and here that make boat traffic on the St. Lawrence River not possible. If this were Germany, we would build canals to bypass them."

"This will never be Germany!" Jack snapped. I saw him stiffen in his chair.

"Oh, Jack, please ... no offence was meant. It is just that our country is old and we have conquered our rivers. And, as an engineering professor, I find the rapids of professional interest. Have either of you been to this place ... this Cornwall?"

"Never," I said.

He opened the drawer of his desk and pulled out a ruler. He placed it against the map. Then he put a finger at the end and moved the ruler to the other side of his finger.

"It is no more than 250 miles. With a fast car it could be done in five hours."

He looked up and seemed almost surprised we were

there, as though he had got so caught up in the map he'd forgotten about us.

"Your arm," Otto said, pointing at Jack. "You no longer have the cast!"

Jack smiled and held his arm slightly aloft. "I got it off yesterday. I can't believe how white my arm looks." His other arm was tanned from the summer sun.

"You must be pleased," Otto said.

"Really pleased. Now I can do things again," Jack said.

I hadn't actually noticed it slowing him down at all. In some ways I was sad to see it go. Wearing the cast was almost like a reminder of what could happen if things went wrong—almost like a warning sign on the road. Now, without that sign to slow him down, there was no telling what Jack might do.

There was a sharp knock at the door and Hans poked his head in.

"*Einen Moment, bitte, mein Kapitän ... in privat.*"

"Excuse me." Otto got up, circled his desk and left the office, closing the door behind him.

"What's that all about?" I asked.

"Probably about the newspaper. Go and stand by the door and listen," Jack said.

"Wouldn't it be better if you went? You know more German than me."

"I know a lot more German than you, but I've got other things to do."

Jack stood up and walked behind Otto's desk.

"What are you doing?" I demanded.

"Isn't it obvious? I'm looking on his desk."

"But you might get caught!" I whispered.

"There's *less* chance of me getting caught if you stand guard."

He was right. He was wrong to be doing what he was doing, but he was right about it being safer with me on the lookout. I jumped to my feet and went to the door. I could hear them talking.

Out of the corner of my eye I watched as Jack lifted the map and looked at the papers underneath. What did he think he'd find there—especially if it was written in German and he only had a few seconds? This made no sense, and—I heard footsteps coming closer!

"Jack!" I leaped back into my seat as the door opened, but there was no way Jack could get back in time! He had turned around and was looking out the window as Otto came back into the room.

Jack turned his head. "You have a really nice view," he said.

"It is nice if I do not look too far into the distance. Then I can see the fence and the guard tower. Even a beautiful cage is still a cage."

Jack walked around his desk in one direction while Otto walked around in the other. They both sat down.

"There is one more thing we need to discuss," Otto

said. He pulled a wallet out of his pocket. "I had said, what ... ten dollars for the map?"

"You said five, but we don't want that," I said. "Our mother would kill us if she found out we took money."

"Your mother knows about this map?" he asked. He sounded concerned.

"No, we didn't tell her," Jack said. "George meant that Mom wouldn't want us to take money from somebody who's treated us so well."

"Yeah. Just think about all the ice cream we've eaten," I added.

"Sharing that with you has been my treat. Here," he said as he pulled out a five-dollar bill. "You must take it or I will feel badly."

"I don't know," Jack said.

"But I do." Otto reached over the table and practically stuffed it in Jack's hand. "If you did not take it I would feel badly if I were ever to ask you for things again."

"We only have the one map," I said.

"One map is sufficient. Other things ... things that may seem silly but would be of interest."

"What sort of things?" Jack asked.

"A ticket, even used or torn, from a theatre."

"Why would you want that?" I asked.

"The ticket stub would help our theatre company make a ticket that looked more Canadian for our production. Other things would just be souvenirs for when we go

home—trinkets, dry-cleaner tickets, flyers or advertise-
ments. Picture postcards showing places like Niagara Falls.
Stamps—even cancelled stamps—for our Stamp Club."

"I didn't know you had a Stamp Club," I said.

"Oh yes. And there are other things. You have no idea
how much we miss the simple pleasure of reading a
newspaper."

"Newspaper?" Jack said. "I have one right here in my
bag." He opened his bag and pretended to look around
for a newspaper he knew wasn't in there. "It's not here.
Maybe it dropped out when I dumped the mail." Jack
started to get up. "I'd better go and—"

"I shall see. Stay seated!" Otto said as he jumped to his
feet. He hurried out the door.

I looked over at Jack questioningly—why had he done
that? Bill would be really mad if he'd gone to all that work
and we ended up with the paper instead of the prisoners.

"It is here," Otto said as he came back into the room,
waving the paper over his head. He handed it to Jack.

"Thanks. It's the Toronto paper. I bought it at the store
today ... but you can have it if you want. I can always get
another one."

"That is so kind of you."

Jack offered the paper but pulled it back. "But why
don't they let you have newspapers?"

Otto shook his head. "I really do not understand. The
paper is censored, so it does not seem to matter. It is not

as though there are secrets. Most of the men would just like to know who won at hockey—many of the men have become fans of the game, very exciting. Others like to do the crossword puzzle—it helps with English lessons."

"I guess there's no harm in you having a paper," Jack said. He offered the paper again and Otto took it. "They don't always have the Toronto paper, but I can get you the *Bowmanville Bugle* if you want."

"Any paper would be good. And those other items— silly, I know—but if you could bring them in . . .?"

"We can bring some of them for sure," I offered.

"Yeah, we can try," Jack confirmed.

"Maybe we should go and get that ice cream now," Otto suggested.

I wasn't about to turn down ice cream, even if it did feel a bit creepy now, knowing that Otto was just using us to get what he needed for the escape. It was harder to feel friendly toward him, easier to remember that he and the others were our enemies in this war.

"We'd better get home," Jack said. We have to cut the lawn before supper."

"But we just cut it a few days ago," I said.

"And it's growing fast so we have to do it again."

"I didn't know."

"Now you do." Jack got up and I followed him.

"See you tomorrow," I said.

I trailed Jack out of the building.

"You really are stupid," Jack said to me.

"What are you talking about?"

"First off, don't mention Whitby ever again, understand?"

I nodded.

"And second, if I say the lawn needs to be cut then just agree with me."

"I just didn't know it had to be cut."

"It doesn't," Jack said. "We needed to get home as soon as possible is all. We have to talk to Bill about all those things that Otto wants."

"Those things didn't make any sense. Why would he want a dry-cleaning ticket?" I asked.

"I don't know, but Bill will, and that's what I want to find out."

CHAPTER FIFTEEN

IT WAS STRANGE being at the camp at night. It wasn't that it was dark—the lights on the fence kept the compound brightly lit—but it was ... different.

Jack and I walked up to the gate.

"Coming for the show, are we?" Smitty asked.

"I hope it'll be good," I said.

"I 'eard the last one was a sight to behold," he told us. "Everyone's makin' a big to-do about it. Lots of important folk are 'ere."

"They are?" I asked.

"Colonel Armstrong, a few high mucky-mucks and the mayor of Bowmanville—they're all inside already."

"We're not late, are we?" I asked. "The ticket says it starts at eight and it's not even seven-thirty yet."

"It's four minutes *after* that, and I know that one for a fact 'cause my relief is late again and I'm supposed to be 'eading 'ome for me supper!"

"Maybe you should stick around and see the play," I suggested.

Smitty started to open the gate. "I 'ave no need to see a bunch of Germans speaking old English, and butchering it to boot, prancing around up on no stage! 'Sides, them prisoners stays on their side of the fence and I stays on my side of the fence and everybody is 'appy."

"Enjoy your supper," I said.

We were let in through the second gate and proceeded across the compound. There wasn't much activity, but the prisoners we saw were in their dress uniforms, and their boots were shined. We exchanged greetings—a few words, nods of the head or waves—with those that we knew.

"I'm not sure I'm going to enjoy this," I said to Jack. "I'd rather just go to the movies and see a Western than some play."

"You and me both," Jack agreed.

"But I thought you really wanted to come tonight."

"Not to see the play," he said.

"Jack, we're not going to do anything stupid ... right?"

"I never do anything stupid— Hey, there's Otto."

Otto was standing at the entrance to the hall where the play was being performed. He was standing beside the field marshal, and as prisoners went in they saluted the two men. They were both in their dress uniforms, all sorts of medals and decorations plastered across their chests.

"Hello, Captain Kretschmer," I said. It didn't seem right to call him Otto when he was dressed up and wearing all those medals.

"Good evening, boys. And where is your dear mother?"

"She couldn't come," I said. "She wasn't feeling good."

"Hopefully nothing too serious," he said. He sounded concerned.

"It's a headache. She gets them sometimes," Jack explained.

"But she takes this medicine and it knocks her right out," I added. "She's dead to the world for the night, and when she wakes up she feels better."

"She's probably asleep right now," Jack said. "She won't even wake up when we get home."

"Hopefully she will be having pleasant dreams. Let me walk you to the door."

He said something in German to the field marshal and guided us up the stairs.

"I am so glad you could come tonight," he said.

"We're glad we could be here," I replied.

He opened the door. "I have always enjoyed our times together." He paused. "Now I must return to welcome guests. I am afraid that the best seats are already taken."

"We'll find something," I said.

There was a soldier just inside the door and he asked for our tickets. The tickets were modelled after one—

ripped in two——that we had given Otto, telling him it was from a play we'd seen two years ago. We had, of course, gotten the torn ticket from Bill.

We'd also given him some postcards, and cancelled stamps, and a number of newspapers, and those dry-cleaning tickets. Every time we brought something in I'd sweat my way through the gates. Jack tried to convince me we really had nothing to worry about because, in the first place, nobody ever searched us, and second, what could they say even if they found the dry-cleaning ticket in my pocket? I knew what he said made sense, but the feeling in the pit of my stomach had nothing to do with logic.

Bill had explained to us the significance of the different objects we were bringing in. Most were items that an escaped prisoner could show to military police if he were stopped, to "prove" that he was just a regular guy with a history on the outside.

We moved into the hall. It was crowded, packed with folding chairs arranged in rows. Most of the seats in the centre were already filled. Off to one side, near the front, we saw Colonel Armstrong, along with three other uniformed officers we didn't know and three men in suits——probably one of them was the mayor.

"Did you hear what he said?" Jack asked quietly.

"Otto?"

"Of course. Did you hear what he said?"

"That he was glad to see us but all the good seats are taken—"

"Not that!" Jack muttered. He motioned for me to follow him into a corner away from the crowds.

"He said he always enjoyed his time with us."

"Yeah? So he likes being around us. I like being around him, too."

"He didn't say *enjoys,* he said *enjoyed* ... like in the past, like it was over, like he wouldn't be spending any more time with us," Jack explained. "Don't you see?"

I shook my head. "He probably just got the two words confused in English."

"He speaks English better than we do. I just wonder if something is going to happen."

"Tonight?" I asked.

"Maybe tonight. Maybe tomorrow before roll call," Jack said.

"Are you sure?"

"Of course I'm not sure. If I was, we'd get out of here and contact Bill."

"Then what *should* we do?"

"We stay and watch."

That sounded reasonable. I was afraid he was going to suggest something risky.

"How about if we sit there?" I suggested to Jack, pointing to two seats in the centre about halfway back.

"How about if we sit right here?" He pointed to two solitary seats off at the back by themselves. They were directly in front of a curtain that blocked the light coming from a side exit.

"But that's a lot farther away. We won't be able to see as well from there."

"That's where you're wrong. We'll see even more from there than we ever would from the middle rows."

I didn't agree, but I didn't feel like fighting. Especially since I really didn't care whether or not I saw the play. After all, maybe Shakespeare sounded better the farther away you got. We settled into our seats. Quickly the other seats started to fill.

"Look at the orchestra," Jack said.

There were close to fifty musicians—the prisoners' symphony orchestra—all together in front of the stage.

"Do you see who's playing the trumpet?" Jack asked.

"There are three trumpets and ... it's the accordion player!"

"Keep it down!" Jack whispered.

"I hope he plays the trumpet better than he plays the accordion."

"I don't care how he plays. The important thing is that if he's here, he can't be sitting outside House Four," Jack said.

Dozens of times over the past few weeks we'd seen him sitting outside that house, playing the accordion.

There was something going on—we were sure of that—but something we couldn't put our finger on.

The hall continued to fill until every seat was taken and the balcony, where everybody was standing, was filled to overflowing. Below the stage was where the orchestra was set up and the musicians were tuning their instruments. It was a funny combination of racing scales, melodies and disjointed notes. It was somewhere between music and mayhem as the different chords and notes sounded out.

"How much longer before they start?" I asked over the din.

He looked at his watch. "It's one minute before eight, so count on it beginning in one minute. You know how the Germans are about being punctual."

I did know. I got the feeling they'd rather be on time and wrong than late and right.

"Looks like everybody in the whole camp is in here," I said.

Jack leaned close to me. "That's what I'm hoping for."

"What do you—?"

Suddenly the lights went out and the audience noise hushed. There was complete silence, like everybody was holding their breath at once. The orchestra jumped into the void and the music swept through the darkness. Up front the curtain opened. A lone figure walked onto the stage and the audience began to clap.

Jack tugged me by the arm to get my attention. He then slipped out of his seat and dropped to the floor, crawling away into the darkness and disappearing through the curtain covering the exit. Anxiously I looked around. None of the few faces I could see were looking in our direction. Nobody had noticed. I dropped to my knees and crawled off for the curtain after him. The darkness was both disconcerting and reassuring. I flattened myself against the floor to push through the curtain, hoping it wouldn't even flutter as I passed by.

There was more light—it was still dark, but not pitch-black. Now Jack was standing at the bottom of a short set of stairs. Behind him was a door, and light was flowing in through the glass at the top. Silently I made my way down.

"This isn't smart," I said. "We shouldn't be doing this."

"*We* don't have to. I'm going to check out House Four, but it's probably better if I go by myself."

"How do you figure that?" I asked.

"One person can move faster than two. Besides, if somebody notices I'm gone you can make an excuse for me."

"What sort of an excuse?"

"Tell them I had to go to the bathroom, or I was feeling sick, or how Shakespeare bores me. The last one wouldn't even be a lie."

"I don't want to be in there by myself," I said reluctantly.

"Then just come with me. Nobody is going to notice anything until intermission and we can be back by then if we leave now. Are you coming or what?"

I knew the smart thing to do. I also knew I wasn't going to do it.

"I'm coming."

Jack put his shoulder against the door and it groaned loudly. I practically jumped out of my skin. He opened the door just enough to get through. I squeezed through after him. Jack bent down, picked up a stone and put it in the door jamb so the door was held slightly ajar.

I looked around the compound. We were partially hidden in the shadows of the building and protected by some bushes. I didn't see anybody. A ring of lights clearly marked the fences, and within the compound, like spokes on a bike, the paths linking the buildings were illuminated. We'd have to avoid the fences and the paths.

Jack moved around the auditorium. We couldn't risk going anywhere near the front. We'd have to make a wide circle that would take us past the playing field and behind the dining hall. Not everybody was going to be in the theatre, but it was a pretty safe bet they wouldn't be at either of those locations at this time of night.

We skipped across a path and ran onto the playing field. It was dark and empty. The fence and three different guard towers were clearly visible from where we were, but there was no way the guards could see us—at least, I was almost certain we were invisible. And anyway, if they did see us, what would they care? People were allowed inside the compound. The eyes of the guards would be focused where their lights were aimed—on the fence and the gate. That was a little reassuring.

We left the field and darted across another path, stopping when the shadows of the dining hall hid us. We were now only two buildings away from our objective: House Four. Jack started around the building in one direction and then skidded to a stop.

"Do you see somebody?" I whispered anxiously.

"Better to circle around on the side away from the tower."

"But the guards aren't going to be looking for us," I said.

"Maybe not, but there's more light coming from the fence, so there's more chance of somebody, anybody, spotting us."

I trailed after him. He was right, it was darker on the far side of the building. As we rounded the building I saw the corner of House Four. Beyond it were the fence and guard towers. I turned around and looked back at the rest of the compound. House Four was definitely closer to the fence than any other building. Why hadn't I ever noticed that before?

Jack walked out of the shadows, ran across the path and came up to the side of the building. I sprinted after him, not daring to stop until I was pressed against the side of the building too.

"This is the way in," Jack said, pointing to a door just off to the side. He sidled over and reached for the door and pulled. "It's locked."

I knew Jack was disappointed. I felt relieved.

Suddenly the door burst open and three soldiers came out. They were talking loudly and laughing, and then all three began singing energetically and off-key. I froze to the spot, pressed against the building, as they walked across the grass to a path and headed toward the dining hall, the sound of their singing gradually fading. Finally it was quiet again.

"That was close," I said. "I don't know how they didn't see us."

"They wouldn't have noticed if they'd tripped over us," Jack said. "They were all drunk."

"Drunk?"

"Couldn't you tell?" Jack asked. "Makes me wonder if they have a still in there."

"Do you really think so? Maybe that's what they were protecting. If that's all it is, we could head back—we don't care if there's a still."

"You're right, we don't, but I think there's more here than any still. Let's keep going."

"Look, the door didn't close behind them!" Jack said. It was slightly ajar. He reached for the door and pulled it

open. He stepped in, holding the door so I could slip in
after him. We were facing a long hallway. There was a
bare light bulb dangling from a wire at the far end, but
other than that the hall was dingy and dark.

"Do you hear anything?" I whispered.

Jack turned his head and listened. "Nothing. Do you?"

"Just my heart beating."

Even in the dim light I could make out Jack's scowl
quite clearly.

Silently we walked down the hall. We passed by doors
on both sides—doors that were, thank goodness, closed.

"What are we looking for?" I whispered.

"I'll know when I see it."

The farther we went down the hall, the closer we got to
the light bulb and the more exposed I felt. Jack stopped as
the hall opened up into a bright sitting room. There were
chairs and tables, and I could picture lively games of skat
going on there. Now it was empty and quiet. On the opposite side of the open area another hall led away to the far
end of the residence. That was the end closest to the fence,
the end that was always guarded by the accordion player.

On silent feet Jack started across the sitting room. I
followed close behind, turning my head from side to
side, scanning all around. Jack stopped and I practically
bumped into him.

"Why did you—?" I started to say, and then I heard
voices. I looked to the left just in time to see the front

door start to open. Jack and I both jumped forward, just making it into the far hall before anybody could appear. We ran down the hall—all we had to do was get to the door at the end and we'd be outside—and two men appeared out of nowhere, blocking our way! They looked shocked to see us as we skidded to a stop.

"Hey! Halt!" yelled one of the men.

"The other way!" Jack yelled as he pushed me back.

I'd run no more than a few feet when I saw two men blocking that end of the hall as well. We were trapped!

"Halt! Stop!"

Jack grabbed the doorknob of the door to our right. He shook it, but it was locked. The men were rushing toward us from both directions! Jack pushed on the door on the other side of the hall and he practically tumbled in as it opened. I jumped in over top of him and—

There were three men, all wearing filthy clothes, standing in the little room Their expressions looked as shocked as I felt. A fourth man appeared out of nowhere, his head and shoulders popping out of a hole in the floor.

There was a rush from behind as two men shot through the door and I was grabbed!

CHAPTER SIXTEEN

I WORKED HARD to control myself. I didn't want anybody to see me trembling even though I was terrified. I bit down on my cheek to chase away the tears that wanted to escape. My clothes—my *good* clothes— were now streaked with mud from when we'd been grabbed. What was Mom going to say when she saw my clothes? I suddenly realized how ridiculous it was for me to be worrying about that. I had other things to worry about.

I rubbed my left shoulder. It had been wrenched and twisted by the one soldier when I'd tried to wriggle free. There really hadn't been any point in fighting. They had us outnumbered, out-muscled and trapped in this little room—the room where the tunnel started.

Jack sat in the chair beside me. I knew he was trying to look brave, but he looked scared. On either side of us stood a soldier. Two more stood directly behind. All were in the same filthy clothing, faces blackened, hair caked with mud. We sat there and watched as another dozen men came out of the opening—all equally filthy, all equally shocked to see us as they exited the tunnel.

They talked among themselves quickly and quietly in German. I couldn't pick out enough words to make any sense of what they were saying. Jack probably understood more. I didn't *want* to understand more. I just wanted to be somewhere else.

The door opened and Otto appeared. He was still in his fancy dress uniform, his chest dotted with medals. I expected him to be angry. Instead he looked worried.

"Are you boys fine?" he asked. "You did not get hurt?"

"We're okay," I said, although I kept rubbing my shoulder.

"This is so unfortunate," he said. He pulled up a chair and sat down right in front of us.

He turned to the soldiers and barked out something in German. They all saluted and left the room, leaving the three of us alone.

"You of course know what is happening here," he said.

"We know there's a tunnel," Jack said. "That's pretty obvious."

He stood up and walked over to the hole. It wasn't very big—not much more than two feet square—but it was completely black, hinting at just how deep it might be. He peered down into it.

"The tunnel extends for almost three hundred feet. From here, under the fence, beneath the road and well into the field beyond so as not to be seen from the guard towers."

"Where did all the dirt go?" I asked.

He pointed up. "It is all stored in the rafters of this building. Above our heads are thousands and thousands of pounds of dirt."

"Was that a smart place to put it?" I asked.

"Compounding the risk, the supports used in the tunnel—which are, I am told, no more than four feet apart—are made from wood taken from the attic."

I looked up at the ceiling. Was it sagging or was that just paint peeling off?

"Judging from your expressions, it appears that you two also doubt the wisdom of that. I had my concerns, but so far ..." He shrugged.

"The tunnel is very well lit. All along the tunnel there are lights, although they are turned off now. The electrical system of the residence was diverted. We have also made a ventilation system. Cans from food were taken, both ends cut out and then connected with duct tape. A hand pump sends fresh air throughout. I am told it is very efficient."

"Told?" Jack asked. "It sounds like you haven't been down there."

"As I told you, I do not like closed spaces. It is not a wide path. It must be less than two feet across to fit between the holes the guards have drilled to check for tunnels."

There was a knock at the door and I practically jumped out of my seat.

"*Kommen Sie,*" Otto said.

The door opened and another soldier in dress uniform appeared. "*Fünf Minuten,*" he said.

"*Ja, ja,*" Otto answered, and the man left.

"Only five minutes until intermission ends, and I must be seen to arrive or suspicions will be raised." He paused. "I was just wondering, what made you suspicious of this house?"

"The accordion player," I said. "Did he play whenever somebody got too close?"

Otto smiled slightly and nodded. "Before I leave I must apologize," he said. "It is my fault you are caught up in this ... this ... pickle. I should never have invited you tonight, and all would have been well if your mother had been here to watch you." Again he stopped talking. He looked unsure of what he was going to say next. "I have enjoyed our time together, and I simply wanted to say goodbye."

"You're going out tonight. You're going to escape, right?" Jack asked.

He nodded again. "I will be leaving just after lights-out at eleven. Myself and Field Marshal Schmidt. It has been requested that we escape."

"Requested by who?" I asked.

"Requested by our superiors."

"But you two are the highest-ranking Germans in the camp," I said.

"*Ja,* but this request is from outside the camp."

I remembered that he'd met Hitler, that he'd been personally decorated by him, and had an eerie vision of the führer himself ordering them to escape.

"They built this whole tunnel for the two of you?" Jack asked.

"We will use the tunnel first. Four hours later, once we are clear and away, then others will follow. Many, many, many others."

I felt a charge of electricity shoot through my body. This was what Bill had been afraid of, what we were supposed to be looking for—what we'd discovered too late and were helpless to stop.

"It is best that I go now—"

"Wait. What's going to happen to us?" Jack asked.

"You will be our guests tonight."

"You can't just keep us here," Jack said. "When we don't get home, our mother is going to call Colonel Armstrong and he'll search the camp."

"Your mother will sleep until the morning. You told me that."

"But when she wakes up and finds us gone she'll call right away," Jack responded.

"And in the morning is too late. Everybody will be gone."

"Will we be released then?" I asked.

"I will personally see to your release," Otto said.

"But ... but ... you won't be here," I said.

"And neither will you boys."

"What do you mean?" I asked.

"You will be coming with me ... through the tunnel."

CHAPTER SEVENTEEN

THE PLAY HAD TO HAVE FINISHED by now. I looked at my watch. It was almost ten-thirty. That meant that it wouldn't be long until Otto came back ... until we went into the tunnel.

"Could I get up?" I asked one of the prisoners guarding us. I sort of knew him—at least we'd talked a few times before all of this and he'd always been friendly. Nobody seemed that friendly now. "I just want to stretch my legs," I explained.

He hesitated and then nodded.

I got up off the chair. My legs felt numb from sitting so long. Actually my head felt numb as well. I'd been straining, trying to understand what was happening, struggling to think of something we could do. Nothing. We were caught. We were trapped.

I walked over until I was standing just above the hole in the floor. I looked down. From this angle it was no longer dark. I guessed they'd turned their lights on. The hole got wider just below the floor and there was a ladder leading down. At the bottom another hole headed off—toward the fence and the field on the far side.

"Can I get up too?" Jack asked, and he was given permission. He sauntered over to my side.

"You okay?" he whispered.

"Been better."

"Just stay alert," he said quietly. "I don't know how or when, but a chance will come. When that happens you just run ... understand?"

"No more talking!" one of the guards barked.

I looked at Jack, nodded and mouthed the words, "I'll be ready."

The door opened and Otto, followed by Field Marshal Schmidt, entered the room. They were both dressed in dirty coveralls. Otto had another pair—no, two pairs— over his arm.

"Please slip these over your clothing," he said as he handed them to us. "Your mother would not be pleased to see your good clothing ruined."

I took the pair and slipped my leg in, my left shoe sticking in a spot before it popped out the leg hole. I pointed my toe and the second leg went through without a hitch. I put my arms in and buttoned up the front, then rolled up the extra-long sleeves and legs.

The field marshal had already started down the hole. He had to rotate his shoulders to fit them through the opening.

"Jack, you will proceed next, then George and then myself," Otto said.

Neither Jack nor I moved.

"Please, it will be all right ... you must trust me."

"Trust you?" Jack scoffed. "You're the enemy!"

Otto shook his head. "I am not the enemy. I am your friend, and I safeguard your lives."

"What does that mean?" I asked.

Otto walked over to the hole and looked down. He walked back to our side.

"Your discovery of our tunnel was considered an act of espionage."

"We weren't spying," I pleaded.

"Please, George, we all know better." He paused. "Do you know how spies are treated when they are captured?"

I did know. They were shot.

"To leave you here is to risk your lives. I convinced the field marshal—who is my commander—that you could be helpful to our escape."

"There's not a chance in hell we're going to help you," Jack said defiantly.

"Just by being with us you offer assistance. They will be less likely to stop men travelling with their children. And if they do stop us, we will have two hostages."

Hostages! We'd be hostages!

"Jack, it is time. You go next."

Jack didn't move.

"Please, Jack, I do not wish to leave you here. It would be too dangerous. Down the ladder."

Jack hesitated for a split second and then walked over to the hole in the floor. He started down the ladder, step by step, slowly disappearing into the hole.

"Now you, George."

I didn't want to go, but I didn't want to stay, either—especially without Jack. I went to the hole and started down. Jack was waiting for me at the bottom.

"As soon as you get out of the hole at the other end get ready to run," Jack whispered in my ear. "There's only the field marshal and he's old. I'm going to knock him down. You have to run for it."

"But what about you?"

"Don't worry about me. Somebody has to warn the guards. Somebody has to—"

"Is everything all right?" Otto called down the hole.

"Sure. Everything's okay!" Jack yelled back. "My brother is just nervous about going in the tunnel. I told him he'll be fine—he just has to follow me."

"Good! Listen to your brother, George. Do as he says and everything will turn out for the best!"

Jack nodded at me. "Just be ready. I'll tackle the field marshal as soon as I see your head pop out."

Jack dropped to his knees and then disappeared into the rectangular opening. I got down on my knees and peered into the passage. It was well lit, with a series of lights hanging from a wire. I could clearly see Jack moving along. I could also see the wooden supports—the wood taken from the attic of the building—at regular intervals. They were keeping the tunnel from collapsing ... collapsing and burying anybody who was in it at the time. How many feet of earth would be over my head, and how much would it weigh if it fell in and——?

"It will be fine, George," Otto said as he reached the bottom.

I nodded.

"I will not allow anything to happen to you boys. You have my word of honour."

"Really?" I didn't know what to think about Otto any more. And as for honour, was that something I could really count on from an enemy?

He nodded.

"I'll go." I didn't see that I had any choice. I ducked my head so I could fit into the tunnel opening. Somehow it had seemed bigger when I was just looking at it. I felt my whole body get hot and sweaty. Was there enough air down here?

"George," Otto said. He was kneeling right beside me. "I do not like this either, but there is no choice. Move, bit by bit, and you will soon be out. You must move."

He was right. I put my head down and started crawling. How long had he said that it was ... three hundred feet? That wasn't long, about the length of a football field. All I had to do was keep my head down and keep moving.

I looked in front of me. The tunnel dipped down and moved slightly to the right. I couldn't see where it went. I stopped moving. Then I realized that I couldn't see Jack any more. I was more scared to be left behind than I was to go forward. I started moving again. Besides, if Jack was going to do what he said he was going to do, I had to get as far ahead of Otto as I could. The farther ahead the better the chance I'd have to escape. Maybe I could even help Jack when it was time to jump the field marshal—he wasn't that big and he was pretty old—and then the two of us could get away. I doubled my pace.

The tunnel started to slope upward. That had to be a good sign. Then I felt cool air ... a breeze. There was air flowing in from the far end. I passed by a light and saw that there were no more lights ahead. The illumination from this one stretched out ahead, getting dimmer and dimmer. Why wouldn't they have strung out a few more lights, since they'd gone to all this trouble? Then it hit me. I had to be so close to the end of the tunnel that they couldn't risk light leaking out, showing the exit.

I turned and looked behind me. Otto was well down the tunnel. He was too big to move as fast as I could. I was soon going to be through and able to help Jack before Otto could help the field marshal. This might work out. I tilted my head up to try to catch the light that remained and crawled as fast as I could. I came to the end. There was a ladder leading upward.

I stood and put a hand on the ladder. I looked up. The opening framed the stars in the sky. It looked pretty ... but I didn't have time to stand there any longer. Otto was behind, but he'd be here soon. I started climbing. There were only a half-dozen rungs. I stopped just before my head poked out. I needed to just catch my breath, ready myself for what was going to happen, whether it was fighting or running. I heard sounds coming from beneath me. Otto was almost at the opening too.

Okay, it's now or never, I said to myself.

I grabbed the top rung of the ladder and practically rocketed out of the opening. Jack was standing right there alongside the field marshal. He just stood there, doing nothing. Why wasn't he doing something?

Then I saw the darkened figures of two other men, guns in hand, standing above me. It was the guards! They'd discovered the tunnel and we were safe!

"Schnell! Schnell!" one of the guards said as he reached down, grabbed me by the arm and pulled me through the opening.

"It's okay, it's me!" I screamed. "I'm not a prisoner! I'm—"

There was a sharp pain in the back of my head as something smashed against my skull and ... everything went black.

CHAPTER EIGHTEEN

"GEORGE? GEORGE, can you hear me?"

I tried to sit up but I felt woozy all over. I opened my eyes. It was dark and I couldn't focus.

"George, are you all right?" It was Jack.

"I don't feel so ..." My stomach did a big flip and I knew I was about to be sick. I slumped forward, my head between my legs, working hard not to vomit.

"Are you fine?" I looked over. It was Otto.

"What happened ... where are we?" I stammered.

"We are in a car," Otto said.

I forced my eyes to focus. Jack was sitting on one side of me, Otto on the other. In the front seat there were three men, one of them the field marshal, and we were hurtling down a dark country road.

"But the tunnel ... the guards were there."

"Not guards," Jack said. "Germans ... Nazi agents."

My head felt so foggy. How could any of this be?

"They were sent to bring us to safety," Otto said. "They hit you when you started to scream. I was so worried ... so worried that they had hurt you badly."

"I thought you were dead," Jack said.

I reached up to the aching spot on the back of my head. It was tender to the touch and swollen.

"You were out for a long time," Jack told me.

"How long?"

"Close to two hours. It's almost one in the morning."

"I just hope Mom is sleeping or she'll be worried to death," I said.

"I hope she's awake and she notified the camp and they're searching the compound for us right now," Jack said. He turned to Otto. "That'll be an end to your plans to have the other prisoners escape."

Otto shook his head. "Those plans have changed ... been rescheduled."

"What do you mean?" I asked.

"Originally the second wave was not to start their escape until we were far gone. We were to have a four-hour head start. Instead, there are already men in the tunnel, waiting only until the stroke of one to begin leaving."

"How many men are going out?" I asked.

"There is no harm in telling you now. It will be over three hundred men."

"Three hundred!" Jack exclaimed.

"We have been planning this as long as we have been digging the tunnel," Otto said. "Over sixteen months of preparation. Planning routes, preparing false papers and identification and making civilian clothing."

It was at that instant that I realized that Otto was not in either dirty coveralls or his uniform. He was dressed in a suit and tie. He didn't look like a prisoner or a German soldier.

"But even if hundreds of people do get out, how far can they get anyway?" Jack asked. "They're all going to be recaptured."

"There is no question that escape is most difficult. Almost all will be found, but it will be a massive undertaking requiring thousands and thousands of your soldiers. And who knows, some may even make their way back to Germany."

"Not a chance," Jack said, and he snorted. "They'll all be caught."

"Perhaps. Although without realizing it you boys have made their escape more possible."

"Us?"

"I wish there had been another way," Otto said. "I feel badly that I tricked you. Those things you brought into the camp. Those little articles of daily life were part of the escape plan. If one of our men is stopped and searched and can produce a few tokens, such as dry-cleaning tickets or a movie stub, he can try to prove he lives in Toronto and is not an escaped prisoner. It might be enough to fool a checkpoint or a search."

So he'd been gathering that stuff, just as Bill had said he would. Maybe *that* was what he was hiding in that bag he always carried arround.

"So we brought you a couple of stubs, so what?" Jack said.

Otto had figured us for spies because we'd found the tunnel, but obviously he had no idea how far our involvement went.

"We used those few things to reproduce samples for all the escaping prisoners," Otto said. "And of course those stamps and postcards you brought were invaluable. We used those to send correspondence—uncensored—to our contacts. They were mailed when prisoners were out walking. We made a promise to return, but said nothing about dropping a postcard into a letterbox. That is how everything was arranged ... like this ride."

I didn't know what to say. None of this was really any surprise. Bill had told us exactly what all those things would be used for. But if Bill had seen all this coming, why were we in a car hurtling through the Ontario night, while back at the compound hundreds of prisoners were starting to crawl out of the tunnel? Their escape plan had worked, and rather than helping to stop them, we'd aided the enemy.

"You're all going to get caught," Jack said again. "Unless this car can fly or float, you're not getting back to Germany in this thing."

"You are correct. This car can only go so far ... but we hope it will be far enough. Now, it is time for sleep. Put your heads down and try to rest."

My head was hurting and I felt groggy. Maybe if I did close my eyes I could blot out what was happening and try to forget the role we'd played in helping it all to take place.

I started thinking about my bed, in my bedroom, in my house, with Jack asleep in his bed down the hall and Mom in her room, just a call away. I started to feel a warmness creeping through my body. Maybe I could sleep a little.

I awoke with a start, not knowing where I was. I looked around, unable to make sense of my surroundings for a second, until it all came back in a rush. I was in the back seat of the car. Jack was lying down beside me, a slight whistling sound coming out of his nose as he slept. Four men—Otto, the field marshal and the two agents— were standing in front of the car, a map stretched across the hood, flashlights out, loudly discussing something. Were they lost? Was it the map we'd brought into the compound? Maybe the changes Bill had made to it were causing the problems.

As I watched, one of the men bundled up the map, the flashlights were turned off and the four men climbed back into the car. They were talking—arguing—loudly, in German. The four doors slammed. Jack startled and sat up.

"What's wrong?" I asked Otto as he settled in beside me.

"The map ... crazy map ... it does not correspond to the signs along the road. The signs show one way and the map shows another. These distances are wrong, and we cannot afford to be late."

"Late for what?" I asked.

"Our rendezvous. Our meeting."

"Meeting with who?"

Otto didn't answer at first. I could see from his expression that he was thinking things through before speaking. "At this point there is no harm in telling. You were correct, this car cannot take us to Germany, but we will be meeting something that can."

"A plane or a ship," Jack said.

"Not a ship," Otto said. "A submarine."

"But you can't get a submarine into Lake Ontario. You said that yourself," I said.

"You can have one slip into the St. Lawrence River and go as far upriver as the first rapids near Cornwall."

"That's why you were interested in rapids, to see how close it could come," Jack said.

"We are racing to that spot to meet it. We must be there before sunrise or it cannot risk surfacing."

"And if you don't get there in time?" Jack asked. "Does it leave without you?"

If that was the case, maybe all wasn't lost—maybe that stupid map would be enough to foil their attempt.

"It delays things. We stay hidden until the next night," Otto explained. "That greatly increases the danger of discovery, although with hundreds of prisoners free around Bowmanville I do not think anybody will be searching for us this far away."

I felt my sense of hope deflate. He was right.

"Even if you get to the submarine, what makes you think that it can get back down the St. Lawrence without being detected?" Jack asked.

"It got upriver without being seen."

"But nobody was looking for it," Jack argued.

"Nobody will be looking for it on its return, either," Otto said. "Nobody will know to look."

Jack looked over at me, and I knew we were both thinking the same thing. Two people would know—my brother and me.

"I was not wishing to inform you earlier than necessary," Otto said, "but it will not be possible to release you when we board the submarine."

"What are you going to do with us?" I asked, afraid of what he was going to say.

"There is no choice," he said. "You boys will be coming onto the submarine with us."

"Onto the submarine?" I asked, astonished. "You're not serious ... are you?"

"If the Canadian authorities knew we were travelling by submarine, we would have no chance to make a run down the river," Otto said. "We cannot leave you on the shore to inform them."

"There has to be another way," I said.

"There is only one other way, and that I will not consider," Otto said.

"Maybe you *should* consider it!" I pleaded.

He shook his head. "Your death is not an option I will contemplate."

"Death?"

He motioned to the front seat. "That was considered. The plan now calls for you boys to stay with us until we reach the Atlantic Ocean. Then, if a safe time and spot can be found, you will be put off in a dinghy close to shore."

"So we'd only be with you a few days?" I asked hopefully.

"If all factors go well."

"What could go wrong?" I asked.

"We might come under attack. The submarine could be destroyed," he said calmly.

I could imagine what it would be like to be in a submarine with depth charges exploding and pipes starting to leak, and then the whole submarine lurching forward, throwing me against the bulkhead with water pouring in——I'd seen enough war movies to picture it far too clearly in my mind.

"But there are other factors. We can only surface to allow you to leave if we are certain that we are clear of enemy ships and the sea is calm enough."

"You can't surface in rough seas?" I asked.

"We can surface, but I cannot allow you boys to be placed overboard unless I am certain that conditions will allow you to reach shore safely."

"We're willing to take that chance," Jack said.

"But I am not. You are in my charge and I must ensure your safety."

I almost didn't want to ask the next question because I was afraid of the answer. "If ... if you can't put us off ... what happens?"

"You will be returning with us to Germany."

"Germany!" I cried.

"There is no choice. You will be my guests."

"You can call us guests if you want," Jack said, "but we're still prisoners. We'll try to get away, to escape."

"I expected that reply. It would be both foolish and dangerous to try. For now, let us just hope none of that will be necessary."

The car began to slow down, and then it practically squealed to a stop before making a turn down a darkened dirt road. I looked through the front windshield. I couldn't see anything except the gravel road and ditches captured by the beams of the headlights. The driver barked out a few words.

"We have arrived," Otto said. "And with time."

CHAPTER NINETEEN

I WAS SHAKING. It was cool, and the breeze off the water was strong, but that had nothing to do with it. Waves were gently lapping against the shore, and the sound was almost reassuring. Above, the sky was littered with thousands of twinkling stars. The new moon was a darker circle in the dark heavens, adding no light. That was probably all part of the plan—the escape timed for the darkest night to help avoid detection.

Otto, the field marshal and one of the agents stood at the edge of the water. The agent held a signalling device, and at intervals he was flashing a light out over the empty water—a river so wide that the other side was lost from view in the darkness. There had been no return signal yet. Behind us, at the place where the beach met the trees, stood the second agent. He was staring, stony-faced, a pistol in his hand.

"This might be our last chance," Jack said softly.

"Maybe there isn't a submarine out there. Or maybe we're not at the right spot," I said, thinking about the false map.

"We can't count on that. We have to make a break for it."

"A break where?"

"Only two ways to go," Jack said. "Left and right."

I looked up the beach in one direction and then the other. Smooth, open sand, broken by a few scattered pieces of driftwood, disappearing into the darkness. There was nothing to hide us and no place to run to.

"I figure if you go one way and I go the other he can't catch both of us," Jack whispered.

"He has a gun. He doesn't have to catch either of us."

"He's not going to want to use the gun. The sound of gunfire might attract the authorities."

"Are you sure?" I asked.

Jack didn't answer. Obviously he wasn't that sure.

"Even if he doesn't fire at us, there are two of them. One could chase you and the other could come after me."

"They'll never catch us. Once you make the trees you'll vanish into the bush. Whoever gets away has to get help. We have to contact the police or—"

Jack stopped mid-sentence. He'd seen what I had just seen—a flashing green light from across the water. Was it the submarine ... was it out there?

"It's now or never," Jack said.

"I suggest it be *never*," said a voice from directly behind my shoulder. I turned around. The second agent was standing almost on top of us. He held a pistol at waist level, aimed right at where we stood. "You would get no more than three paces," he said. "I am a crack shot. The captain has asked that we not kill either of you boys, and I will follow orders … unless I am given no choice. Run and there will be no choice."

"We're not going to run," I finally said, although I was talking to Jack as much as I was to the agent.

"To the water's edge now," he said, motioning with his gun.

We started walking down the beach and he trailed right behind, his gun at the ready.

Out on the water the light came again. This time it was blue—three flashes of blue. The agent holding the device signalled back with two bursts of green. It had to be some sort of code. Almost immediately three green flashes appeared from the water. He changed the coloured filter and replied with two blue bursts.

"Signal that there will be two additional passengers coming aboard," Otto said. He turned to us. "I know this is not as you would wish. It is not as any of us would wish. But it is as it must be. You will be treated well and returned if possible."

"Word of honour?" I asked, looking for reassurance.

He nodded. "My word of honour as an officer and a gentleman."

I knew what that meant, and I felt a little bit calmer. Otto was a German captain, a soldier of the country we were at war with, but he would keep his word.

The calm night air was suddenly shattered by a loud hissing sound coming from across the water.

"The submarine is surfacing," Otto said. "It is blowing the water out of its holding tanks."

I strained my eyes, trying to make out the submarine's form in the darkness. I couldn't see anything on the water, or ... wait ... I saw something ... or thought I saw something. Way out in the river, well away from shore, a dark shape started to rise above the water. Because I knew it was a submarine I could tell it was the conning tower. The sub rose higher and higher until the deck of the ship surfaced as well. Off in the distance it didn't look that big. Either the submarine was smaller than I'd imagined, or the distance was disguised in the darkness and it was farther away than I thought.

Another series of lights came—red, then green, then blue.

The agent fiddled with the signalling device. He flashed two reds, then two greens and finally two blues.

"Only a few minutes now," Otto said. "Take off your shoes and your socks."

"We're not going to swim out there, are we?" I asked.

"Not to fear, George. A rubber raft is coming out to shore. It is better not to have on shoes in case of a tumble over the side."

I felt relieved ... and scared. The submarine surfacing in the distance had seemed almost like an odd curiosity, like it wasn't real or wasn't something that had anything to do with us. Now, with the rubber raft coming, it was all too real.

I started shaking more, and I knew that tears weren't far behind.

"Jack, when we get in the raft I want you and George to work the paddles and the rudder," Otto said.

"We're not going to help you escape," Jack said. "We've already done enough stuff we shouldn't have."

"It is not to help me. I want you to have a practice run. Hopefully the next time you are in that raft you will be rowing for shore in the Atlantic Ocean."

"Oh ... sorry," Jack said. "Thanks, I guess."

The agent flashed the signal again. A simple white light. There was no answering light. He signalled again. I realized he was probably only showing the raft our position on shore. He continued, every fifteen seconds or so, with another burst of light.

"There it is!" Otto exclaimed.

Small and low to the water, I saw a darker shade of black coming straight for us, slowly getting larger as it approached. There were two—no, three men. Two were rowing and the third sat at the back steering.

When Otto yelled out something in German the two men stopped rowing and turned around. The momentum of the boat carried it toward us and the man at the rear of the raft threw out a bright yellow line. It flew through the air, landing short of us in the water. One of the agents waded into the water up to his waist, grabbed the rope and towed the raft toward shore.

As they closed in, the two sailors jumped into the water as well and the three of them pulled the rubber dinghy up onto the sand.

The two sailors saluted, and Otto and the field marshal returned their salute. They started speaking quickly in German. I couldn't understand anything. They were talking too fast, and I was too overwhelmed to even try to pick out the occasional word. Besides, what was the point? Nothing that I would hear could help me.

I glanced over my shoulder. The second agent continued to stand behind us, pistol at the ready in case we might use these last few seconds to make our break. I had no intention of even trying. We were caught. There was no escape. No hope.

Suddenly the whole sky exploded in a blaze of light and I put my hand up to shield my eyes! There were flares in the sky, dozens of them, and lights were racing across the water from all directions.

"Drop your weapons!" screamed a voice behind us. I heard branches crashing and feet running and there was movement all along the beach. Then I heard the sharp crack of gunfire!

"Get down!" Otto yelled.

Before I could even think to react he smashed into me and Jack, knocking us off our feet, causing us all to crash into the sand. I tried to fight but I was pinned under his weight.

"Do not move!" he shouted. "Keep your head buried in the sand! Do not move!"

I started to struggle when another great weight dropped on top of me. It felt as if my rib cage was going to collapse. I turned around ... it was the agent ... his mouth and eyes wide open, blood pouring out of a gaping hole in his side! I looked away.

"Nobody move! Nobody move!" yelled a voice—a voice with a thick English accent.

Within seconds we were surrounded by men, dozens and dozens of men, all dressed in black, with woollen hats over their heads, faces blackened, carrying rifles—rifles that were aimed at us.

The agent's body was pulled off and two sets of hands pulled me to my feet and then threw me, face first, to the ground. A boot slammed into my back. I watched, sprawled out on my gut, as the field marshal, the other agent and the three sailors, all standing with their hands in the air, were swarmed and knocked to the ground as well.

Behind them the water was churning with activity as boats, with bright lights blazing, criss-crossed the water. The submarine was gone. No, not gone, it had dived below the surface. There was a mighty explosion and a plume of water shot high into the air. Depth charges. They were dropping depth charges! Then there was another explosion and another and another. They were trying to destroy the submarine or drive it to the surface.

"Let them up," a voice said. I knew the voice. It was Bill!

The boot in my back lifted and somebody reached down and took me by the arm, helping me to my feet. The others were helped up too, and then the eight of us—me and Jack, the field marshal, Otto, the agent and the three sailors—stood in the centre of a large circle of men, all with weapons aimed at us.

"We're so happy to see—"

"Not a word from you, kid!" Bill yelled angrily. "I don't know who you and this other boy are, but if you've helped the enemy you'll be shot!"

"But … but …"

"They were not aiding us," Otto said. "They were taken as our hostages from the camp. This was all against their will."

"And why should we believe you?" Bill demanded.

"Because I speak as an officer and I give my word."

"We'll make our own decisions," Bill said.

"You knew all along, didn't you?" Otto asked him. "This was all a trick to get the submarine, yes?"

"I'm not here to answer your questions. You just stand there and—" His words were cut off by a thunderous explosion, much louder than the others.

"We got her!" somebody yelled. "That has to be a direct hit on the submarine!"

I looked at Otto. He'd know better than anybody if that was true. His face was a mask of grief and distress.

The surface of the water was shattered as the submarine jumped out. The whole side of the vessel seemed to be ripped open, and there was smoke and fire. The boats closed in from all sides.

I knew this was good, that they had captured or destroyed an enemy submarine, but I also knew that most likely people had died—that still more people were going to die tonight. I knew they were Germans. I knew they were our enemies. I also knew they were people. People with wives and children and families. People like Otto. I couldn't bear to watch. I looked away.

"The two boys come with me!" Bill ordered loudly. "The others will remain under guard on the beach!"

Two men grabbed me roughly by the arms, while two others did the same to Jack. We were half marched, half carried, my feet barely touching the sand, behind Bill, across the beach and toward the woods. Reaching the protection of the trees, Bill stopped and turned around.

"Release them," he said.

He walked slowly back toward us. He looked angry.

"You realize that you two almost got yourselves killed ... *again?*"

"I'm sorry ... we're sorry ... it all just happened and there was nothing we could do and they had guns and—"

"George," he said as he stopped me by putting a hand on my shoulder, "I understand." He paused. "You boys scared the living daylights out of me," he said. "Thank goodness you're okay."

He wrapped an arm around my shoulders and the other around Jack's and pulled us toward him, and all the tears I'd been fighting to keep inside came flowing out as I buried my face in his chest. It was over. It was finally over. We were safe.

CHAPTER TWENTY

"YOU HAVE TO GET GOING," Bill said. "Little Bill is waiting for you in his car."

"Little Bill is here?"

"He was directing the entire operation. He waited on the beach, just beyond the bright lights, until he was certain that the operation had been successful."

Bill led us along a trail through the forest. It ended at a roadway. There were three large army trucks and two cars parked at the side.

"His is the first car, the larger of the two," Bill said. "I'll talk to you boys later."

"You're not coming?" I asked.

"I have matters here that need to be attended to." He turned and walked back into the forest, leaving Jack and me standing by ourselves.

"You through bawling like a baby?" Jack asked.

I sniffed back my tears.

"You notice you're the only person here who was crying?" Jack asked.

"You notice that I'm the only twelve-year-old here?"

Jack nodded ever so slightly. "How's your head?"

"Still attached to my shoulders ... just the way I like it."

"Let me have a look." He pulled me over, spun me around and looked at my lump. "Could be worse—they could have hit *me* in the head."

I tried to pull away, but he held on tight. "Seriously ... you okay?"

"I'm okay now."

"Good. Let's not keep Little Bill waiting any longer."

We walked over to the first car. It was big—long and black. The windows were dark and I couldn't see inside. Jack knocked gently on the glass. The back door opened slightly and a little light came on inside the vehicle. Jack pulled the door open and I peered in. Little Bill was sitting on the back seat. He was dressed, as always, in a suit.

"Good evening, gentlemen. Fancy meeting you here. Please," he said, gesturing to the seat beside him.

Jack gave me a little shove to get me moving. I climbed in and took a seat beside Little Bill. Jack sat down beside me. Little Bill leaned forward and tapped on a window that separated us from the driver. The window slid open and a man's face appeared.

"Drive," Little Bill said. "Please."

"Yes, sir," the driver said, and the window slid shut again. The engine came to life and seconds later we started moving.

"Where are we going?" I asked.

"Bowmanville. I'm driving you home."

"Oh, it'll be so good to get home … I'm so tired, and we have to get there before seven when our mother wakes up and finds we're not there. She'll be so worried and—"

"We can't get there that quickly," Little Bill said, "but she won't be worried."

"Of course she's going to be worried."

"It's been taken care of. Late last night we had an operative break into your house … although technically he didn't break in since the front door was open. You should lock your doors."

"But why did you send somebody into our house?" I asked.

"He rumpled your beds to make them look as if they'd been slept in, left dirty cereal bowls and glasses in the sink and a note on the table stating that you'd been taken up to the camp—at the request of Colonel Armstrong—to do some work. She'll never know you weren't there."

"I guess that'll work," I said, "but we're still going to be in big trouble."

Little Bill looked confused.

"We're not supposed to leave the house until our beds are made and the dishes are cleaned up," Jack explained, and Little Bill laughed.

"Could we ask you a question?" I said. I wanted to ask the same thing Otto had asked Bill.

Little Bill nodded his head. "Certainly."

"Their plan ... the escape ... did you know all about it?"

"Not everything, and certainly not the most important thing."

"What was the most important thing?" I asked.

"We didn't know where the submarine was going to rendezvous with them. We had to let them lead us there, and they did."

"So you let them get away on purpose?" Jack asked in amazement.

"Yes. Although their plans apparently called for well over three hundred men to escape ... that we didn't allow. Within ten minutes of your escape the tunnel was guarded at both ends. A team went into the camp and found the suits, disguises and false identification that had been produced."

"But ... but ... how? How did you know about things?" I questioned.

"We were intercepting the messages they sent in their letters. They were communicating using a code called Ireland. A prisoner sends a letter to his wife. It seems like an innocent account of life in the camp. However, the first letters of all the words, when put together, form the real message. Reading the letters was like reading a progress report on the tunnel."

"But Otto told us they also sent some messages using the postcards and stamps that we gave them," I said.

"The stamps and postcards *we* gave to you to give to them. We watched those being mailed and intercepted them as well."

"Why didn't we know about any of this?" I asked. "Why didn't Bill tell us?"

"Standard practice. We only give operatives the information they need to do their part of the job."

"What I want to know," Jack said, "is, if you knew so much about their plans, why didn't you just stop them?"

"Stopping them wouldn't have got us the submarine. We wanted that U-boat. That was the real prize."

"And you got it."

"Yes, we did. And we were fortunate that the price wasn't too high."

"How could it be too high?"

"I was afraid it could cost us your lives," Little Bill said. "If I had known you had been abducted, I would have stopped them immediately."

"But you had to know. You were watching the escape, weren't you?"

"My men were—from the trees across the field. All they saw in the dark were four people coming up from the tunnel. We assumed four prisoners."

"Didn't your men see them slug me?" I asked.

"That incident was reported. I must admit it confused me. However, we still didn't know who it involved. It wasn't until much later that we started to have our suspicions that you two had been involved."

"What tipped you off?"

"We had two operatives at the performance. They were guests of Colonel Armstrong."

"We saw them," I said, thinking back to the two men in the suits who sat beside the man I thought was the mayor.

"When I spoke to them a few hours after the escape— they were coordinating the capture of the tunnel—they mentioned that you were at the camp. Yet when I checked with our outside observers there was no record of you two having left. Then I thought, if anybody could get themselves entangled in this mess, it would have to be the two of you … and there you were … and here you are now."

We rode along in silence for a while.

"We almost fouled things up again," I finally said.

"Again? You never fouled them up before."

"But we came close both times."

"You were a part of the team that made things possible. Without you boys, things might have turned out differently. You have been of great service to your country ... once again." He paused. "And once again, no one can know."

"Like no one knows what you or the other men at Camp X do."

"It must remain secret. For us all."

"I understand," I said. "The important thing is that *we* know what we did."

"And that's enough?" Little Bill asked.

"It is for now ... and for the next time you need us. We'll be ready."